MERCILESS RIDE

Hellions Motorcycle Club

CHELSEA CAMARON

MERCILESS RIDE

A Hellions Ride

HELL RAISERS DEMANDING EXTREME CHAOS

USA TODAY BESTSELLING AUTHOR

Chelsea Camaron

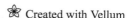 Created with Vellum

CONTENT WARNING

This book contains strong language, strong sexual situations, violence, and sexual assault. Please do not buy if any of this offends you.

This is not meant to be a true or exact depiction of a motorcycle club rather a work of fiction meant to entertain.

STAY UP TO DATE

D o you want to get bonus scenes, sale updates, new release information and more?
Click here to sign up for my newsletter!

W ant to get an email direct to you with every new release or sale?
Follow me on Bookbub!

C onnect directly with me anytime at:
www.authorchelseacamaron.com
Facebook
Twitter
Instagram

ALSO IN THIS SERIES

Hellions Ride Series:
One Ride
Forever Ride
Merciless Ride
Eternal Ride
Innocent Ride
Simple Ride
Heated Ride
Ride with Me (Hellions MC and Ravage MC Duel with
Ryan Michele)
Originals Ride
Final Ride

HELLIONS RIDE ON SERIES

MERCILESS RIDE

Mercy is no friend of mine. Karma, she has yet to show kindness to me.

The hits keep on coming for Tessie Marie Harlow. She has never known easy. Her mom is disabled, her dad long gone, and she is a single mom raising a rambunctious little boy who is her world. Finally giving up on a future with Rex, Tessie comes to terms with her reality.

One night changes everything.

In the darkest hour of her merciless ride through life, she's saved by a quiet, laid-back Hellion.

Andy "Shooter" Jenkins is a former Army Green Beret. He has always been around, yet he has never been one to stand out in a crowd and he's never loud. He is a mystery.

A chance encounter brings him to her rescue, not once but twice.

When the Desert Ghosts motorcycle club bring their brand of chaos to Tessie's world, Shooter is forced into her day-to-day life.

Secrets are revealed. Lines are crossed as a war between the two clubs begins. Two brothers find themselves at odds at a time when they need to work as one.

Hellions Ride Series Reading Order:

One Ride

Forever Ride

Merciless Ride

Eternal Ride

Innocent Ride

Simple Ride

Heated Ride

Ride with Me (Hellions MC and Ravage MC Duel) co-written with Ryan Michele

Originals Ride

Final Ride

LETTER FROM CHELSEA

Dear Reader,

Please note this book takes place with the Catawba Hellions charter therefore you will not see some the regular Haywood's Landing Hellions. The timeline of this books slightly parallels that of Forever Ride so you won't have Tank and Sass as they are off in their story during this particular book.

Shooter and Tessie are on a ride of endurance and self-discovery. Hang on as this is a ride where secrets will be revealed.

Much Love,
Chelsea Camaron

DEDICATION

DEDICATION

To Author Theresa Marguerite Hewitt

My writing partner, my critique partner, but most of all my friend. You inspired Tessie's character and you are one of the most amazing people I have ever met! Enjoy the ride, sweets.

To Amazon Reviewer Dusty Rose

I don't even know if you will read this, but you posted a review for One Ride and mentioned Tessie. She was originally a support character not meant to have her own book. You inspired me to give her a ride of her own. Thank you for your honest feedback. Thank you for being the old lady behind the man in the cut (your review says you're a real old lady so my helmet off to you—I ride with my husband and my father, but they are not one percenters—that's a tough life and world to live in as a woman. You are a strong female and I tried to give Tessie what I imagined to be your strength to persevere.)

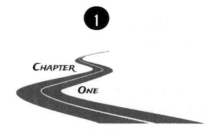

UNEXPECTED

No, no, no, don't die, dammit. Fuck my life.

It is two in the morning, I just got off work from the bar, and tonight has already been a long damn night. We have been busier since the Desert Ghosts Motorcycle Club arrived in town. They must be working with the Hellions on something to be here, returning as often as they do.

Staying in this small place, they only have two

options for a spot to grab a beer. *Tiny's,* where a man that is far from tiny will be serving them, or find me and the girls at *Ruthless.* Since they are in business with the Hellions, they come to *Ruthless.* Although not Hellion owned, it is known as their place to grab a drink and unwind.

I am on my way to pick up Axel, my son, when my little Honda Civic begins dying a slow, painful death as my dashboard lights up like a Christmas tree. I have just enough time to pull it safely to the side of the road before it shuts off completely.

No! This can't be happening; I think to myself as I try to restart the car.

Turning the key over in the ignition, I am left with silence surrounding me. Click. Click. Click. Nothing.

Looking over at my cell phone, I think of my limited options for aid. Who can I call at two in the morning to come give me a ride?

I don't want my mom to have to get dressed and then get Axel dressed to come out here. Plus, I am still going to need to have the car towed. I knew I should have signed up for one of those automotive clubs, but damn that would be another bill. A bill I certainly can't afford.

Picking up my cell phone, I dial the one person I know that can help me get a ride and get my car towed all in a quick manner as well as keep it within a reasonable budget.

"Hey, Doll, sorry to call so late," I say when she answers.

"No problem; what's wrong, Tessie?" she asks, the sleepy tone in her voice reminding me normal people don't keep my kind of schedule.

Shit, I woke her up. I feel even more guilt now, but she is one of the few friends I have. Plus, she will come get me, no question, since Tripp and Rex are away on a transport. I would've been tempted to call Rex; however, I have promised myself no more. Luckily, he is away, so the urge is gone, leaving me with Doll. If they were home, Rex would've been at the bar tonight, either to troll for fresh pussy or give me an orgasm in the stock room before the night was over. Rex and I have a fucked up history - one centered around sex, sometimes a little more, but mostly it is just about getting off. Well, that was until recently when I made the decision to cut him out of my life as much as possible.

"My car broke down out on Miller's Hill Road. It won't start back up and I need to get home. I'm sorry for bothering you. I didn't know who else I could call," I say as I hear a noise in the background.

Doll is mumbling something, but I can't bring

myself to focus on her as my blood runs cold when I hear Tripp's voice say *his* name.

Shit, Rex! He can't come get me. No. No. No. He cannot come with me to get Axel. Panic is setting in as I run through how this night is going. He will ask me where my son is. He always asks me about Axel. My plan was to get Doll on her way and call my mom to keep him overnight. If Rex is too close, I won't have time to make the call. Then he will wonder why we can't go get him.

"No worries, Tessie, Rex will be there shortly to get you," I hear her say his name, snapping me out of my thoughts.

"Rex? I th… thought they were on a transport," I stammer, questioning why he is back.

"Oh, they got back about an hour ago. Tripp heard you talking so he called him while we've been on the phone. He'll pick you up and get your car taken care of. Do you need a ride tomorrow?"

"No, Doll. Thanks, you've done so much already. I gotta go. I need to call my mom so she's not expecting me right away for Axel." With that, we hang up.

Making a quick call to my mom, I ask her to keep Axel overnight for me. Since he's already asleep, this works out better for him anyway. Regardless of who comes, none of the Hellions are going to lay eyes on Axel.

Knowing my son is settled, I have to prepare myself to see Rex. I seem to lose all self-control when he's around. I always have. Boundaries, I have given myself mental boundaries with him. He is never going to grow up, so I have stopped holding out for that. He is also never going to commit to me or anyone else, for that matter. I have given up on that pipe dream. With that said, I have to set the boundaries for my body more firmly. No more allowing lust to takeover.

Rex is sex walking, period, end of story. He has shoulder length, dirty blond hair. Eyes that are piercing blue, a body that's got defined muscles, and ink that makes you want to lick every inch of his skin. The thing about Rex, he knows he is the whole package. He knows he looks good. He's confident in his bedroom abilities, as he should be. There is also this edge to him. The same edge that all the Hellions carry. The thing that draws the barflies to them like a man lost in the desert to water.

Headlights coming my way draw my attention. Then a wrecker pulls up in front of my little car. I hold my breath as the driver side door opens, my mouth dropping open when it's not Rex who climbs out.

At six feet tall, with broad shoulders and all muscle, the man coming to me is another example of the edge all the Hellions carry. His long-sleeved, black T-shirt pulls tightly against his well-defined chest, abs, and arms. His normally spiked blonde hair is hidden under an old, worn out, baseball hat. The jeans he is wearing are well washed and fit him like a pair of broken in shoes, comfortable perfection. Black motorcycle boots stop in front of me, drawing my attention back to my situation.

"Hey, Tessie, let's get you loaded up and home to your boy."

"Shooter," is all I manage.

"Yeah, baby, you get me. Rex called. He couldn't make it, but didn't want you on the side of the road."

This is the moment my heart should sink a little that Rex isn't coming to help me. What surprises me, though, is I don't feel short changed in the least bit. I don't feel let down. For once, I feel absolutely nothing for Drexel 'Rex' Crews.

SHOOTER

Damn him!

Brother or not, right now, I want to kick his ass. I swear I heard him speaking to someone else as I answered the phone, *"Suck it harder, bitch."* Instead of dropping the barfly, he calls me to pick up his woman off the side of the road. Only Tessie isn't his ol' lady; she's just his back up pussy; the pussy he doesn't want to hold onto yet won't let go of, either.

Tessie is beautiful. She deserves so much better than Rex or any man the likes of us. She's petite, maybe five-feet-four, with dark brown hair and brown eyes that dance when she smiles. Her perky breasts are what most may consider small, but they fit her body perfectly. She has a round ass, but not overly large, just enough to really grip as she rides you. With Tessie, though, it's more than that. She is genuine, caring, and sweet. Loyal to a fault sometimes, she puts up with a lot of shit, not only from our club, but all the guys going into the bar.

I won't lie to myself; I have watched her for years with Rex, envious as hell. Tessie accepts him as he is, whatever he gives her. I have never met a woman who can easily understand and take a man truly at face value the way Tessie does, not only with Rex, but all of us.

I have been a patched member of the Catawba Hellions MC for five years now. My boss, Ryder, introduced me to the club after he patched in with the Haywood's Landing charter. His wife Dina's father was an original before he passed away tragically in a car accident years ago.

I make the almost hour commute daily to work at Ryder's Restorations in Charlotte. Most days, I paint cars for him. Occasionally, I step in on some fabrication, but it's rare. The pay is good, business is good, and the guys at the shop are good. I could relocate to a place closer to work, but I don't want to be in the city. I like being close to my club and not having neighbors close by. This life is simple and calm compared to what I have seen in my past.

I am going through the routine of hooking up Tessie's car to the wrecker. My buddy here in Catawba has a towing and recovery business. He said he would come get her, but I couldn't do that to Tessie. She's a single mom, by herself on an old road in the middle of nowhere, and it is beyond late. A familiar face might make things a little better, especially since I don't know how disappointed she is over Rex not coming personally.

Glancing over my shoulder, I see she's watching me.

"Need help?" she asks, sticking her hands in her jean pockets.

"Nah, baby, I got it. Go ahead and get in. I'll be a few minutes, and then we'll get you home."

She nods at me before proceeding to get in the truck. The 1993 silver Honda Civic she has been driving certainly has seen better days. Once we get this to the shop, I'm going to give it a complete over-haul. She has a kid to get home to.

Jobs here are few and far between. The bar is really the only place she could go right now without leaving her mom behind to work in the city. It's a small town, people talk, and Tessie hasn't had an easy life.

With the car secure, I climb in behind the wheel to tow it back to my place. Looking over to the passenger seat, I see she has fallen asleep against the door already. Reaching over, I buckle her in, and she startles and wakes.

"Shooter, thank you."

"Anytime, baby. You need me to take you to your mom's or your place?" I ask, wondering if she needs to pick up her son.

"My house, please. Mom didn't want me to wake Axel."

The exhaustion is written on her face, but more than that there is loneliness in her eyes. I don't know why, yet I feel the need to apologize that it's me that came to get her.

"I'm sorry Rex couldn't make it."

"I'm not," she says, gazing out the window into the dark night.

How do I respond to that? Rather than involve myself in another man's business, I stay quiet. Her phone rings from her purse saving me from continuing our conversation.

"What, Rex?" she answers with a dull tone. There is a pause for him to speak. "Yes, Shooter came. I'm on my way home." Her brows draw together in frustration, but her voice remains impassive. "No, you can't come over tonight." She sighs deeply. "Rex, I told you, no more." Another pause. "You couldn't come get me because you were doing who knows what to some barfly. I'm not stupid. Rex, I told you, I'm done. The fact that you want to come over tonight shows the complete lack of respect you have for me. We're over and have been for years. Hell, we weren't actually ever officially together, so there is nothing to be over."

Her voice never raises, never sharpens. She is calm, cool, and detached as she continues after allowing Rex to reply. "We're nothing more than friends. Move on, Rex. I'm going to. Goodnight." And with that, she swipes her thumb across the screen to end the call.

She lightly bangs her head against the window as we pull up to her house where she starts to unbuckle. Quickly, I reach in my back pocket and get my business card out of my wallet.

"Look, Tessie, if you need anything, I don't care the time, call."

When she looks at the card then up to me, a slight smile crosses her face. "Andy 'Shooter' Jenkins. You look like an Andy."

"What?"

"In all the years you've been coming to the bar, I've only know you as 'Shooter' and 'Jenkins,' never Andy. You look like an Andy."

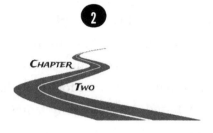

CHAPTER
TWO

NO FRIEND OF MINE

One day I will catch a break. At least, that's what I keep telling myself. Mercy has never been a friend to me. Life just keeps on kicking me while I am down. This is merely another bump in the road, one I will work my way through, somehow, someway.

Looking around my tiny, two bedroom, one bath, single wide trailer that was built back in the sixties, I take in my momentary solitude. To most people, my tiny home would be considered pitiful or pathetic. For me, it's freedom. It's independence. More than that, it is my success. It is mine. This is the place I have worked so hard and saved so much to have for myself and my son, Axel. After giving up everything and starting over, this was supposed to be my reward for all my hard work.

I laugh out loud. Much like my fantasies of Rex one day committing to me, having a place of my own is a mere pipe dream, as well. My mom's health is rapidly declining. At some point in the very near future, I am going to have to face the fact that I should move home.

My mom has Multiple Sclerosis. After battling it for years now, the flares are coming more often and her recovery is becoming longer. My aunt lived with her until recently when she had to move in with my aging grandparents. My mom, seeking to feel strong and independent, asked me to stay at my own place for now. The more time passes, the more I watch the fatigue and muscle deterioration after each flare up.

After my dad bailed, when I was a toddler, my mom put all her energy into raising and supporting me; therefore, she never took the time for herself to find someone else. Then, when she ended up sick, she gave up hope that anyone would want to deal with all her new ailments. That's when my aunt moved in with her after her husband passed away from a heart attack to make sure someone was around for Mom during the flares. This was also their way of making sure I went off to college.

I chose Appalachian State University because they do have a good nursing program and it was still relatively close to home, so I could get back to her if she needed me. I was young and carefree. I wouldn't say I felt invincible, although I definitely didn't think of the consequences of all my actions. They are the very same actions that have me now living in an old trailer with a son I'm raising on my own.

Tears fill my eyes as I think back on the dreams I once had. Dreams I once chased with fervor and passion are now a fading memory in what's become of my life.

A knock at my door startles me out of my musings. There is no peep hole to check to see who is here. No, my tiny, white aluminum sided trailer has a set of three concrete steps leading up to the door that, if I yank hard enough, even locked, will pop open.

The inside of my house is no prettier than the outside. My kitchen has two windows, but one is filled with the window unit air conditioner to cool the small space. The avocado green gas stove and refrigerator are doing nothing to add to the ambiance. I have no dishwasher other than my own two hands, and my counter top has only enough space for the drying rack, a microwave, and a toaster.

The front door opens into my living room that only has enough room for a single couch; no loveseat, no chair, and no table even. Nope, I have a thrift store bought couch that faces two windows and a small television that sits on an old, short book shelf with three shelves.

I never have visitors, except for the time I let Rex come over when my mom was keeping Axel. Looking around, I am embarrassed to show anyone my meager belongings. I don't have pictures on the walls because no frame ever seems to look right against the old, warped wooden-looking paneling. Axel is still young, so I don't put pictures in frames on the book shelf. It's functional for storing his toys.

Down the narrow hallway is Axel's room that is so small it doesn't fit more than his twin size bed. Between his room and mine that is at the end of the house is a small bathroom that happens to be nothing more than a tub, sink, and toilet. I don't have a washer and dryer; I take my laundry to Mom's house weekly. I have what I need to get by. My home is home to me, but it's bare and far too small for others to visit.

Sighing, I pull myself together, pushing back my embarrassment as I open the door. Never in my life did I expect *him* to be on the other side. No, I figured it would be Rex or Doll stopping by, not Shooter.

The door is one that opens outward, not inward like homes of today; therefore, Shooter must step down to the bottom step to avoid the door.

Why is he here?

SHOOTER

S he is standing in the doorway, staring at me with a perplexed expression. Giving her a minute, I remain on her bottom front step, waiting for her to greet me or move to welcome me in. Rather than open the door farther like one would normally do, Tessie steps out onto her top step while holding the door knob in her hand.

Taking her silent cue, I back away until she can come down the narrow three steps and close the door behind her. She watches me intently and obviously doesn't know what to say.

"Hey, baby," I greet to end our awkward standoff.

"Um... Hi, Shooter," she replies, while looking down at her perfectly red painted toe nails.

"I came to drop off my car for you."

"What?" The shock of my statement shows clearly

in her features. Her brown eyes open wide, staring at me as if she is unsure if I am real.

Oh, sweetheart, I'm real, all right.

"Shooter, I can't take your car."

"Baby, you need a car, and I have one that I don't drive daily. I'm here to leave it with you until I get your Honda fixed." It is the God's honest truth. I can't, in good conscience, leave her with nothing to get back and forth in, and the Dodge Challenger is not even two years old with less than six thousand miles on it. I don't drive it except for a weekend cruise here and there. I have a small, Chevy S-10 pick-up truck I use for my daily commute if I don't ride my Harley.

Her family is a close knit one. They don't ask for handouts or help, ever. Her mom and aunt step in to take care of Axel; as a result, she has never had to put him in daycare. Hell, only the town doctor and a handful of others have actually seen the kid. If you didn't know Tessie came home from college because she was pregnant, you wouldn't even realize she had a son.

Word around town says her mom's health is getting worse. Tessie needs a car, not only for work, but to get home to her mom and Axel if need be. I have a car I am not using; therefore, the logical thing seems to be leaving it with her. Too bad her face doesn't show her agreement with my plan.

"Shooter, again, I can't take your car."

"Look, with your car, we gotta order parts. I told you that already. Those take a few days to get in, and I can't leave you with no way to get to Axel, your mom, and to work."

"I'll rent a car," she replies firmly.

"Tessie, don't be stubborn. We don't even know what your car will cost to repair. Take the Challenger."

"Why are you so willing to help me?"

"Call me selfish. If you don't have a car, you can't get to work, and then who would serve me a beer?" I ask in mock innocence.

"Corinne will happily serve you, Shooter."

"Ha. Got jokes, do ya? Corinne will happily serve up more than just drinks. Tessie, I'm just tryin' to be a friend here."

"I would hardly call us friends." Her face is set in stone, not giving anything away. She is tough, but there is a sadness deep in those brown eyes that pulls at me.

"We could be," I state, watching for her to give me some sort of clue or opening, yet she gives away nothing. "Take the car, Tessie."

"I don't need any new friends, Shooter. Keep your car. Thanks for stopping by, but I'll get my car sorted. I'm no trouble of yours."

"Come on, Tessie. Look, I get it, you haven't had it easy. Neither have I, but I have an opportunity to help you, and I want to take it. No strings, no favors, no debts, no markers, just me paying it forward, so to speak."

When she doesn't reply or change her stance, I throw out the big guns. "Okay, I'll call Rex and have him arrange for your transportation." I begin to step backwards, making my exit.

"Wait! You wouldn't really involve Rex, would you?"

"If you don't take the car, yes, I will. Tessie, you're part of the Hellions' family in a way. None of us want to see you struggle. Take the car."

"You won't call Rex if I take the car?" she questions as I watch the determination flash across her face. For whatever reason, she does not want to rely on my brother.

"If you take the car and agree to have dinner with me," I add, totally knowing I'm pushing my luck here.

"Shooter!" she cries out in frustration, losing some of her firm resolve to keep me shut out. "What happened to no strings, huh?"

"What? I want us to be friends, that's all. Seriously, I'm a man with far too much bad history to bring a woman along for my ride, but I want to get to know you as a friend. Besides, I get the feeling you could use a friend right now and just that."

"I'll take the car, but only until my car is fixed. Things are complicated for me, though. I can't accept your dinner invitation. To be honest, it's not in your best interest to be my friend."

As my buddy, Nathan 'Boomer' Vaughn, pulls into Tessie's driveway, I hand her the keys to the Challenger, smiling. "Baby, I've never been one to do anything that's in my best interest. We'll have dinner one night, Tessie. Mark my words." At that final statement, I walk away.

Climbing in the cab of his truck, I look over at my long-time friend as he gives me a shit-eating grin. I shake my head at him.

"Come on, man, that's fine pussy right there." He turns the truck around and drives away from Tessie's place.

"Boomer, don't even go there. She's going through some shit. She needs a friend."

"It's been fuckin' years since Tracie. Let go of the regrets, man."

"Fuck off, Boomer." My tone is sharp enough he knows to drop the subject of my own sorted past.

My past. My regrets. The ghost that holds me back. Tessie should know it's not in her best interest to be *my* friend. This was a bad idea. I will see it through, get her car safe, and slip her some money. But she is right; we don't need to be friends. Tessie needs a good man and good friends, not the black soul I am. I'm poison. I'm a plague to everything I touch. How could I let myself forget it for even one moment?

Tracie's final words haunt me.

"It's you, Andy. You carry the darkness of death with you from the war. You're a trained killer. That's what they've done to you. The man I once knew and loved is now a long lost memory. You keep telling me it's service to my country. No, you're tainted, Andy. You're a killer and you've killed us. I can't take it anymore—what could've been. It's now my blood on your hands, too."

I rub my hands over my face as the final shot rings out through my head. Her blood covered me both inside and out.

After serving my country for nine years in the Army, after selection and training with Special Forces and getting my green beret, my first love couldn't stand to even look at me. The elite, the badass, the sniper, I came home from training, from deployments, from war to my girl's shame in what I had become. It was all too much to bear. The deployments, my nightmares, her knowing what I sometimes had to do without really knowing.

Even though I never told her anything, she made her assumptions. In the end, she took her own life right in front of me. I couldn't save her.

She was the girl next door, literally—my neighbor growing up. High school sweethearts, everyone planned out our lives for us in a way. Only, I joined the Army rather than working in her dad's garage. I took the path less traveled. I did the unexpected. I changed the plan and forced her along for the ride.

She couldn't handle the separation. All that time apart, she was left wondering where I was, if I was safe; all while I was riding an adrenaline high and running off the pride of serving my country. Nothing gained ever comes without sacrifice. My sacrifice in not settling down and having kids for my choice to serve my nation. The cost was much too high for Tracie, a payment she never signed on for. I was trained. I was equipped with tools and coping skills. She was not. She suffered alone. The darkness consumed her until it was all too much to take for even another breath.

The thing is, if she had never met me she would still be alive with two point five kids and a house with a white picket fence: The American dream. That's all she ever wanted. I took it all from her, crushed her dreams and took her life.

Momentarily, I let Tessie's situation cloud my judgment. I was wrong; I can't be her friend. No, I will help her, but then I need to walk away. Rex will eventually stop chasing tail and step up to be there for her. Besides, she's got Doll and Tripp for friends. She certainly doesn't need me and my baggage.

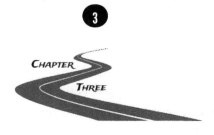

CHAPTER THREE

LIFE

A nother day, another dollar, or at least, that is what I keep telling myself. One day, I will have a regular nine to five job. One day, I will pick Axel up from school, do his homework and have dinner with him, give him a bath, and then settle in for bedtime snuggles. One day, I won't get up from putting him to bed to leave for work. No, one day, I will be able to go from tucking my son in for sleep and crawl into my own bed for the night, as well.

Alas, that is not my current situation. Axel is tucked in for the night at my mom's house. My aunt is staying over so they want him to spend the night. At least I don't have to worry about picking him up after my shift.

Everything has changed and become more complicated. This was all much easier when he was a baby. He is getting bigger now. When he's asleep, he's dead weight to move around and get home.

Arriving at Ruthless tonight, I smile at the bikes already lined up outside. The Hellions prospect, the one who came to pick Shooter up from my place three weeks ago when he left me his car, is outside watching over all the chrome and leather. I kind of feel bad for the guy. Well, any of the prospects, really. They are made fun of most of the time, and the guys run them ragged. It is supposed to be some macho display of dedication and loyalty. I don't get it, but I am not part of the club, so I guess I wouldn't. It's not my place to ask questions or try to understand.

Hmmm… I wonder if he knows when my car will be finished. At this rate, I need to make Shooter's car payment for the month or some shit. It's definitely not something I can afford right now, but I need to pay him, especially if this is going to drag on further. I don't want to owe anyone.

Thanks to Corinne, I have picked up a few day shifts as a waitress at Brinkley's, a local diner. It is nothing to brag about, but it is helping get the bills paid. They have a consistent lunch rush; as a result, I am making a steadier income on tips than I do behind the bar.

The guys are good about slipping me extra, especially Tripp. Rex has tried, but it makes me feel cheap so I always give it back to him. However, I find money pretty regularly in my purse that I am sure comes from him. Since I can't prove it, though, I try to turn a blind eye to it.

I see another biker standing near the bikes, only he is a fully patched member of the Desert Ghosts MC, his cut clearly displaying their insignia. Guess they are sticking around. They have been riding through more and more frequently. Although, in the last two weeks, they have been at Ruthless nightly. Whatever they are here for, they are obviously affiliated and on friendly terms with the Hellions. There is no way they would feel comfortable hanging around this often for this long if it wasn't friendly between the clubs. Hellions run the Carolina's everyone knows it and no one challenges it.

Ruthless doesn't fly official colors. The owner, a good ol' country boy named Bob, says he can't fly colors in his bar while still paying tithes at church on Sunday; he wouldn't feel right about it. Whatever you say, mister. Pastor Joe knows the money placed in that offering plate comes from booze, and that booze was paid for with Hellion's money. He sure doesn't turn it away, now, does he?

Either way, the bar keeps steady business, which keeps me making steady tips. With the Desert Ghosts in town, I have been making a little more each night, saving up to get Axel a trampoline for Christmas, I hope.

Working here, even though I'm surrounded by badass bikers, I feel safe. I know the Hellions won't let anything happen at Ruthless. Sure, we have the occasional bar fight when the brothers get a little drunk. The barflies get in hair pulling cat fights almost nightly, but I feel safe at my job, something I can't say about working at another bar.

The night is busy, and as soon as I get behind the bar, it's chaos—drink orders flying, alcohol spilling, ice dropping, and people shuffling about. The longer it goes on, the more I feel my feet dragging. The extra shifts at Brinkley's are taking their toll. Not knowing what my car repair is going to cost, though, I need every penny I can get.

Corinne rings the cow bell we have over the bar to let the guys know to belly up to the bar and get their final beer then get the hell out. Last call, which means we can go home soon. I am more than ready to hit the bed tonight.

Corinne seems nice enough. She is new to bartending, but definitely not new to bikers. She is a barfly through and through. Although, I guess I shouldn't be so quick to judge. Some people probably think that of me, given my history with Rex.

History, that word again. Well, it certainly is what Rex and I are. Why I ever disillusioned myself to believe there could be more is beyond me.

Rex was the bad boy biker on the streets when I was in high school. He would pass by and wink at me. The first time he spoke to me, we were at a gas station. After I pulled up in my Honda, he strutted over as I was pumping gas. He looked over and saw my high school tassel hanging from my rearview mirror and smirked. It was my senior year. I knew it was cheesy to hang it from my mirror, but I was proud to be graduating and leaving my small town. As he watched me for a moment, his eyes dancing in humor, I was completely enamored and enthralled.

After a pat on my ass, he looked me up and down before saying, "Call me when you're legal." He then walked away with all the confidence in the world, never giving a second glance back. That is Rex, though, never looking back.

Lost in my life musings, the bar is empty before I even realize it.

"See ya tomorrow, Tessie," Corinne calls out as she heads to the front door.

"Night. Drive safe," I reply as I watch her lock the door and walk away.

After turning over the last bar stool, I make my way to the stock room. Sighing, I think back to the many nights Rex would stay behind to close up with me. The many nights he would take me right here in this very room.

Time to let go of all of that, I remind myself. He is never going to grow up or settle down. *Take a page from his book, Tessie, no more looking back.*

SHOOTER

Three weeks.

Three long, fucking weeks.

Ever since Boomer brought her up, the ghost of my past is haunting me once again. She is relentless this time. I close my eyes and see her tear-filled gaze before she pulled the trigger, the depths of her stare begging me to change. Begging me to go back to a time when things were simple between us. Begging me to give up my career and be the man who could be home every night for dinner. The man who could sit beside her at church on Sunday. The man who crawled into bed with her to share my every secret and woke up every morning, cherishing having her in my arms. The stare, the look, and the final moment when she shut down, realizing I could never be the man she wanted. The final moment when I had to accept that I had cost her everything.

When I crawl in my bed each night, Tracie comes to me in my dreams. She reminds me I will never love again. I will never share a bed with anyone. Just as I cost her that dream, she is making sure to take it from me. I wake up drenched in sweat, my sheets soaked to the mattress and twisted into a disheveled mess as I have tossed and turned, fighting the demon within me. I couldn't bring someone else into my nightmare. It would be unfair.

In the end, she got everything she wanted, only she isn't here to share the life she has created for me. I live the life she wanted us to have together. My house isn't as big as she would have wanted, and it is not in a subdivision on a cul-de-sac, but it is a home. I work at the garage where most weeks are a five-day work week, eight hours a day. If we have a rush order, I work late or weekends, but that doesn't happen often. I have my club, but I only go on the transports occasionally when there isn't anyone else to fill in. My Army career is long gone and there is no going back.

Post-Traumatic Stress Disorder that is what they call it. Fucked up beyond any help is what I call it. Either way, I am no longer qualified to do my job. I am no longer one of the elite. My DD-214 lists me with an honorable discharge. My team sergeant and commanding officer didn't want to completely tarnish my reputation, but they felt I was no longer fit for duty. Fit for duty. Hell, I am still not sure I'm fit for life, and it's been six fucking years.

Looking around me, I realize I have lost all control this time. The empty bottles of Jack Daniels litter my space, yet I can't drink the memories away. I have done things I am not proud of. I have killed men. I have seen first-hand the damages of a civil war in a depraved country. I have walked away knowing my job only had a short-term impact and that one day those same, small boys I played soccer with in the street may grow into men who will want to kill me for merely being an American soldier. I have stared men in the eyes, watching them as they die. I have made good decisions and bad. I live with the consequences of my actions, no matter the lasting price I continue to pay. I served with honor, courage, commitment, and pride. And I would do it again in a heartbeat, no second guessing.

My regret is in how I handled Tracie. My job was my job, and I was damn good at it. With all those skills in reading people, I never thought to carry them over into my personal life. I shut Tracie out and took for granted that she would be along for the ride, no matter what choices I made. I was wrong. Dead wrong and that death was hers.

Typically, I can push it all down, put it aside and

focus on day to day activities. When all else fails, I dump my problems in the bottom of a bottle. For these past three weeks, however, I can't escape the memories. I can't push down the thoughts.

I get in the shower, the water turning red in my mind. I watch it swirl down the drain, remember washing her blood spatter and brain matter off my face, arms, and hands. I couldn't get clean enough. I still can't. I am tainted. Her blood covers my soul; it will never wash away. I let her down.

With Tessie's car ready, I have to get my head on straight to deliver it to her tomorrow. Her original problem was her alternator, but not wanting to risk further problems, she now has a new engine, new clutch, and new tires. Reality is, she needs a new car, but I know she can't afford one.

Man up, get the car to her, and let her go. She could use a friend, someone to take her out and allow her freedoms to let go and not feel the weight of the world on her shoulders. That's what she needs, but it can't be me. My demons don't need to spill over into her already fucked up life.

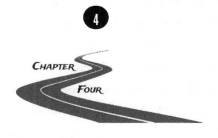

CHAPTER FOUR

SHATTERED

Work. Work. Work. After a busy day shift at Brinkley's, my feet are dragging at Ruthless tonight.

The bar is packed. It seems like the Desert Ghosts have most of their club here tonight. I see Thorn over at the pool tables with Tripp. The Ghosts club prez is not overly friendly. Hell, none of the guys are what I would call nice, whether Hellion or Ghost, but Thorn, that asshole comes off jaded.

He is tall like Tripp, a little over six feet. He has close cut, dark brown hair, almost in a military style cut, and his blue eyes are cold and distant. Out of all the times the Ghosts have come to town, Thorn has been around only two or three of those times; just enough so you know who he is and the power he holds. Usually, it is his brother, Preacher, who happens to be the VP, and a handful of other members that ride in, stay for a few days, and then ride out. Not long after, the local Hellions will take a transport and be gone for two weeks and return again. This is the rinse and repeat type of cycle these guys have going on right now. The few times Thorn has come in, he has come off harsh and abrasive in demeanor. His presence alone gives me chills.

Of course, Preacher is not one who gives off warm fuzzies, either. With him, you never know how the night will go. He is like every other biker: grab a beer, have a shot or two, find a barfly, tap that pussy, play some pool, shoot the shit with the boys, and go the hell home. Other nights, though, Preacher starts spouting off bible verses like it is a Sunday school church program. He's a crazy fucker, that one.

A fist slamming down on the bar causes the glasses

around me to clank, drawing my attention away from the pool table area.

"What, is that bitch too good to serve me?" I hear a gravelly voice ask.

"Tessie is busy working the floor tonight. I'll get you another Jack. Calm yourself," Corinne says in an attempt to calm the drunken man.

"Get my drink then fuck off, barfly."

Damn, Corinne is having it rough tonight, too, it seems. His voice doesn't sound familiar, like one of my regulars, but the bar has been steady lately with the Ghosts, and I haven't gotten used to all of them.

Rex whistles at me, taking my attention back to the pool tables.

Grabbing a tray, I take some beers over to Tripp, Rex, Thorn, and Preacher. Rex pops my denim skirt clad ass. As much as it infuriates me, I know better than to make a scene. Rex is Catawba Hellion VP; he won't take any disrespect from me, or anyone, publicly. Hell, privately he wouldn't take my shit, either. I am trying so hard to break this cycle between us, though. Later, he won't be getting me like he probably thinks he is. No, I am done, and I will be strong enough to stay away this time. Hopefully, before the night is over, he will find a barfly to take care of his needs just so I don't have to remind him yet again that we are finished.

Time passes as more drinks are poured. The night

is continuing on, but the crowd is not letting up. Blowing my bangs out of my eyes with a huff of my breath, I step backwards to grab a rack of clean glasses from under the bar and am stopped as I bump into the body of a man. When arms wrap around my waist from behind, rendering me immobile, I freeze as I recognize the feel of the body behind me. Rex drops his head to my neck and sucks. That bastard marked me.

For the first time in years, my body does not betray me. For the first time ever, I do not melt for Rex.

He comes off my neck with a pop, making sure I know that one will last a few days. "Don't be a bitch, Tessie," he whispers in my ear.

Whispering back to him, I maintain my resolve to keep things over between us. "Having standards for my body is not me being a bitch, Rex." I jerk out of his grasp before he can try anything further.

"Your loss," he simply states as he walks away.

I don't bother to look over my shoulder as I can say, once and for all, I am completely over Drexel 'Rex' Crews.

The rest of my shift finishes in a blur. After our encounter earlier, Rex stays away from me. He spends his evening in the dart area, letting Purple Pussy Pamela suck him off in front of everyone. The fucker just stared at me while holding her bobbing head. So much for me in the grand scheme of things. Am I any better than she is, though?

Rumor has it she went to get a butterfly inked on her pussy, only she let an apprentice practice on her instead of the real artist. She left with her pussy lips being tattooed purple with orange polka dots. *Oh yeah, Rex, let her wet your whistle.*

In the past, I would be on the verge of tears after watching Rex getting sucked off or fucking someone. This is not the first night he has watched me work while getting off by someone else. Tonight, I am not hurt. No, I am angry.

I am angry at him for being the piece of shit, motherfucker he is. I am angry at myself for ever letting him into my life. I am angry at fucking Aphrodite for being the bitch goddess of love who felt it necessary to tie me to this asshole. Karma, yeah, I am angry at her, too. What in the hell did I do to deserve this shit?

"Night, Tessie. I'm outta here, girl," Corinne calls out as she makes her way to the front door.

"Night," I holler back as I round the corner of the bar to head to the back office.

After depositing the cash from tonight in the safe in Bob's office, I head to the stockroom to do a quick inventory to leave a liquor order for the morning. Sighing, I realize this is the quietest part of my entire day today.

The problem with being so damn short is not reaching the top shelf in this storeroom easily. I'm stretching to count when I drop my paper. This night is never ending.

Bending over to pick up my dropped list, I am startled by a noise behind me. Standing up, I don't have a chance to take in what is around me.

Humph.

Smack.

Wetness trickles down my face, though the pain doesn't register right away.

Suddenly, I am no longer bending over to pick up my paper. Somehow, I am against the concrete wall of the back room. Everything is spinning. The uneven surface of the wall cuts into my cheek as someone holds my face in place. One large, calloused palm covers the left side of my face, pushing my right side farther into the grains of the cement block wall of this room, the little rocks digging into my skin, breaking through. His other hand holds my arms behind my back.

My forehead is already bleeding from being slammed against the wall, the wetness continuing to come down. He twists his hand against my face, forcing me to open my mouth in a gasp. My teeth clamp down when he digs the heel of his hand into my jaw. Biting down on the inside of my cheek, my mouth now fills with the coppery taste of my own blood.

Focus, Tessie, fucking focus. What the fuck just happened?

Closing my eyes, I breathe in. He smells of whiskey, stale cigarettes, a mixture of old oil and gasoline, and sweat. He's taller than me, but not as tall as Rex. Exhaling, I try to hold in my tears. *Think, Tessie, think! Dammit, victims die because they lose their shit. Don't lose your shit.*

He feels huge behind me, his weight pressing into me. I feel the design of a cut or vest over his t-shirt and his jeans against my bare legs. Surely, he is not a Hellion, please not one of them.

He will not break me. He will not break me; I repeat in my head as he kicks my legs apart. *I will not cry out*; I remind myself as a whimper escapes.

He presses his hips into my ass, and I feel his erection pushing against me. As his weight shifts, I feel his longish hair as it tickles my bare arm while he drags his tongue from my wrist up my arm.

"Wouldn't serve me earlier, bitch, but you'll serve me now."

That voice. Who the fuck is he? I can't place it.

Inhale.

Exhale.

Survive.

Inhale.

Exhale.

The whiskey engulfs my nose as he breathes over my face before licking my ear, making me shudder involuntarily. This can't be happening. I try to kick back into his shin and make contact. He is relentless, however. His hold never loosens. He pulls at my hair, peeling my cheek from the wall before twisting my head to face it.

Crack.

My head slams back into the wall. Blood pours down into eyes from my forehead. The room spins, darkness tries to consume me. *No. No. No. Hold on, Tessie. Hold the fuck on*, I remind myself right before I go limp.

Coming to, I am still against the wall with my arms twisted up behind my back at an awkward angle. If I move, I am certain I will dislocate my shoulder. His weight feels so heavy against me.

He yanks my skirt up over my ass. Then there's a swift tug and my panties are gone. He grinds against my ass as he licks my shoulder before his teeth sink in. I cry out, unable to hide my pain as I feel him bite down so hard he breaks my skin.

"Please don't do this," I beg barely above a whisper.

Calm down, Tessie, I try to give myself a pep talk.

His forearm presses into my back as he pushes against me, forcing my tank top covered breasts to painfully press against the wall. Then a hand grazes up my inner thigh, his fingers reaching my folds.

Dear God, please, can you find it in you to save me? I know I don't deserve any mercy, but right now, I'm begging for someone, something to stop this. Anything but this. Please, God of all gods, don't let him violate me.

I send up my prayer silently as panic overtakes me. He is too big. I can't fight back. Will he kill me when he's done? If I die, who will raise Axel?

Thoughts swirl through my mind as I try to clench my pussy tight as his finger finds its way inside my core. It hurts. I try to move my hips to get away from his touch while his tongue licks my ear as he pulls his finger out to slam two in me, my inner walls burning in pain at the assault. My body trembles uncontrollably in fear, pure adrenaline shooting through me as I lose control of my limbs.

"Fight it, bitch," his gravelly voice finally comes to the forefront of my mind. He was at the bar tonight, the one Corinne served. "You're so tight. I'm gonna rip you apart."

When his thumb forces its way roughly into my ass, I feel the burn of my puckered skin ripping at his brutality and blood trickle down my inner thigh. My attempt at pulling away only pushes me farther into the wall, my cheek scratching yet again as blood clouds my vision.

Twisting my head, I try to look at him. I can't see him clearly, but I take in what I can. Through my blurred vision I can see his dark hair is slicked back at the roots, but falling at the ends. It is greasy, oily like he hasn't washed it in days. He face is marred, acne scars dimpling it entirely, and there are strange scratches covering under his cheeks and down his chin. What's his name again? Shit! I know him!

His fingers leave my body. Then I feel him shift behind me to drop his pants. This isn't happening. This cannot be happening to me.

The head of his engorged penis is at my sensitive opening, the tip pressing its way inside as he pushes closer to me.

SHOOTER

The sight in front of me can't possibly be real. The Devils Ghosts insignia is all I see at first. Dropping my gaze, I see Tessie's legs spread out with him standing between them. Blood is running down her legs, and he has blood on his arm. My eyes make their way to her face where she is pinned to the wall and covered in blood. Neither of them notice my presence in the small room.

The rage boils in me. Suddenly, all I can hear is her heavy breathing. Drawing my weapon, I don't hesitate to fire. Pop. Pop. I put two bullets in the back of his legs.

"FFFUUUUCKKK!!!" Shep cries out as he drops to the ground where he grabs at his legs, trying to stop the bleeding.

Good luck, motherfucker; you're gonna die.

Whether you bleed out here in this room or my brothers drag you off and take their time carving you up, it doesn't matter. Retribution will be for the Hellions.

Rushing over, I don't give a second thought to him as I scoop Tessie up and remove her from the room. She falls limply into my arms as shock almost certainly sets in. Her ass is bare because her skirt is bunched up around her waist, and her shirt is twisted. My instincts scream to assess her injuries, but there is so much blood I can't see how bad the cuts are.

"Stay with me, baby."

Rushing to her car, I put her in the passenger seat. She is trembling in fear as her body goes into shock.

"It's okay, baby. I'm gonna get you outta here."

"Shooter?" she questions, and I realize she can't see through the blood covering her eyes.

"Yeah, baby, it's me. Hang on, okay. I gotta make a call. Then we'll get you taken care of."

She only nods as her body continues to shake.

Removing my cut, I pull my shirt off and hand it to her to wipe her face. Knowing I shot the fucker in his knees, he's not going anywhere. My inner caveman screams at me to go back in there and finish the bastard off, but I can't do that in front of Tessie. She's been through enough tonight. If I kill him and then she remembers later on... Well, I don't know if that will be something more to haunt her. Blood on your hands, whether actually by your hands or not, still stays with you. Is she strong enough to carry that burden?

She still hasn't attempted to adjust her clothing. Does she not realize she is exposed? I don't dare touch her to fix it, though. Did I get here in time? My mind races. Fuck, how bad is it?

Making the call for back-up, my mind racing, I look over to see Tessie hasn't moved. My shirt still sits in her open hands, her body still shivering uncontrollably.

"Tripp, problem at Ruthless. Shep fucked up Tessie bad. I need Doll and a female doctor to my place Now! Get the boys to come handle Shep. I shot him, so we need clean up," I quickly divulge.

"On it. I'll send a crew and meet you at your house with Doll and Rex."

"Not Rex. That fucker has played enough games with her. Where the hell is he tonight?"

"Shooter," Tripp chastises.

"Not tonight, Tripp. Not fuckin' tonight. She's a mess. Let her make that call."

"All right, brother, on my way."

5

CHAPTER

FIVE

CLAIMED

U gh. Ouch. Everything hurts. Every centimeter of my body is in pain. Slowly, I start to stretch, attempting to open my eyes. They are tight, though; they won't open. Panic fills me as I reach up and touch my face.

Tentatively, I feel around to find my head wrapped in what feels like gauze and bandages on my left cheek. My mouth feels puffy, even on the inside. The taste of old blood mixes with my saliva as all my senses go into overdrive. My anxiety grows as my breathing becomes more erratic. Why does everything hurt?

"Breathe, baby. I need you to breathe."

"Shooter?" I ask, recognizing his voice.

"Yeah, I'm right here." His words are soft, somehow soothing as the fear continues to escalate.

"Shooter, where am I? What happened?"

"You're at my house."

"Wait, your house? Where is Axel?"

Oh, my goodness, was I in an accident in Shooter's car? Is Axel okay? Is he worried about me? Does my mom know where I am? Has someone called her? Who would know to call her? She must be worried sick.

I am reaching around into thin air around me as I still can't open my eyes. Large hands come around my wrists gently, pulling my hands down onto my stomach. I'm still lying flat in a bed.

"Axel is with your mom and your aunt. They know you're okay," he calmly answers me as he releases my wrists.

"Why am I here?" I question, needing to know what has happened.

As he sighs, a delicate, soft hand squeezes my right hand. Instinctively, I jump. How many people are here? I strain to hear more of what is around me. Aren't your other instincts supposed to be more in tune when you lose your sight? Why can I not figure out what is going on? Damn it, I need answers.

"It's me, Tessie. What do you remember?" Doll asks, as she starts to pull her hand out of mine. Knowing it is her, I squeeze, pulling her hand back into mine.

Think, Tessie. Last night or tonight—I don't exactly know what time it is—I went to work. It was busy. Rex was there. He was being an ass. The bar closed.

The bar closed...

I suck in my breath, my body starting to shake uncontrollably as the memories invade. The smell. My God, the smell of that man: oil, cigarettes, whiskey, and leather.

Before I can react, the meager contents of my stomach cover my hands and the bed around me.

The bed shifts beside me as Doll pulls her hand away, undoubtedly to clean it.

I can't stop trembling. He touched me. I hurt; oh, how I hurt. My breathing is coming in pants as the night floods my mind. Dirty. He was so dirty. I am so filthy. His hands, his mouth, his tongue—he was all over me. The dry heaves begin as I have nothing left to vomit, but I cannot control my stomach's revolt.

"Doll, run a bath," I hear Shooter say.

Gagging, I begin to choke causing my breathing to become even more strenuous. I feel his arms rest on either side of me in the bed without touching me.

"Please, breathe, baby. Inhale," he whispers gently. "Exhale... Inhale... Exhale."

I take my strength from him, following his commands to get my breathing under control. One breath at a time that is how you survive. When you can't handle looking so far ahead, think only of one more breath. I feel the wetness of my tears as they escape my swollen eyes and fall down my swollen cheeks.

"We gotta clean you up. Doll is gonna help you. After that, Doc will tend to your wounds. She came last night, stitched your head and checked you out."

"What time is it?" I croak out on a choke.

"Two in the afternoon," Shooter replies in a matter of fact tone, devoid of all emotion.

"Axel," I whisper.

"Baby, he's fine. Remember, your mom and aunt have him. They don't know what happened, just that you are exhausted and need to rest today."

I nod my head. The pain in my body consumes my thoughts as I sit here covered in vomit and unable to see.

Push through it, Tessie, I coach myself. I survived, right? He didn't kill me. Hurt me, yes, but I'm alive.

"I gotta pick you up, Tessie. Doll's gonna help you undress. Doc says the swelling will go down, and then you'll be able to open your eyes and see. Until then, Doll will handle dressing and undressing you. I promise

I won't be in the room. No men, baby. You're safe now."

His concern for my modesty and security is evident as he has yet to harshly touch me or make a sudden movement. My emotional reserve is empty; as a result, I find my calm in Shooter, nodding my head in understanding.

After a bath, with help from Doll, Doc Kelly checks my wounds. She applies some goo to my eyelids to help keep my eyes moisturized while the swelling continues to go down. My nose will have a nasty bump and may possibly need to be reset later, but until the swelling goes down, she can't tell for sure without x-rays. I have vaginal and anal tears that will be uncomfortable as they heal, but much like having a baby, they will be fine in time. Moreover, my concussion will have lasting effects for a while, but eventually, the headaches will go away.

Yes, they all offered to take me to the hospital for treatment if I would feel more comfortable, but that is not going to happen. For me, that would mean answering questions, which would be talking about it and remembering it. I just want to forget. Move on. Wait for the next hit from life.

Mercy could have stepped in to save me last night, yet she didn't. It is more than obvious she has no plans to cut me any slack in the future, either.

Doc Kelly continues to check me over, spouting off

healing times and instructions. She belongs to Head Case. She met him in med school, only he went into mental health while she went into emergency medicine. How they became affiliated with the Hellions, I do not know. She doesn't share, and I don't ask. Honestly, I don't care who treats my external wounds. I have to find a way to get healed and get home to my son. I survived my attack; this is just yet another bump in the road, right?

SHOOTER

SHOOTER

When Tripp calls a sermon, every patched member is in attendance. Boomer is prospecting after my nomination last year, so he is standing outside the cave. I hold no officer position; therefore, I sit in one of the seats along the wall of the tiny space. Tripp takes his seat at the head of the table with Rex, our charter VP, at his right.

The gavel slams down as Tripp calls the meeting to open. He doesn't hold back as he begins, "Tessie was attacked at Ruthless last night."

While gasps and swears fill the air, Rex sits in his chair unmoving, his face never changing as the words sink in throughout the club members that weren't part of the clean-up last night.

"It was Shep from the Desert Ghosts that assaulted her," Tripp adds. "She was closing up alone. Shooter got there to trade his car with hers and found them. He managed to shoot Shep twice and get Tessie out of there, but by the time the boys got to Ruthless for cleanup, Shep had escaped. We've got the stockroom back to normal for Bob, but we have no word on Shep."

I shoot up out of my chair, unable to control myself. "What the fuck do you mean Shep got away?"

"Just what the fuck I said, Shooter. Now sit your ass down," Tripp orders.

Head Case tugs on my forearm to pull me back down to my seat.

"Tessie's not property," Kix speaks up, "so how is this club business?"

"You have got to be kiddin' me," I mutter. "Not property? Tessie's motherfuckin' family. How many of you has she called someone for or taken you home herself because you were too drunk to ride? Not property! She serves every single one of us, at least, weekly. Ruthless is Hellions', and we protect what's ours."

"Ruthless is not Hellions'. Bob won't allow it," Tripp adds, his face stern. "I can't make the call to Thorn to hand over Shep. Tessie isn't ours, technically."

Not thinking, I storm over and pull Rex out of his chair before anyone can react. I pin him to the wall, breathing heavily, eye to eye with him as he grabs at my wrists, trying to relieve the pressure I've got on his throat.

"Claim her, fucker. Claim her!"

I let up just enough for him to make the statement. He doesn't. Instead, he kicks out at me. The shift causes me to let up more, giving him a chance to get room to swing. His fist connects with my jaw. My balance thrown off, I release him. Then, getting myself together, I hit him with an uppercut to the gut. He hunches over, trying to catch his breath, and I take the opportunity, reaching up and pinning him back to the wall, my forearm not closing his windpipe because he is still recovering.

"Enough," Tripp commands.

Spitting the blood out of my mouth at his feet, I give him the biggest disrespect I can in this situation before backing away, watching him for his next move as I return to my seat. Not one of my brothers has moved.

"You gonna claim her, Rex?" Tripp questions his cousin and VP.

He meets my stare as he shakes his head back and forth. "No, I'm not gonna claim her. She's not my property. She's not Hellions' property."

"Not property. You've been tappin' that pussy for years, Rex. Motherfuckin' years! And she's not once been with anyone else that you know of. She's been loyal to you. Where were you last night? Every time she has needed you, where the fuck have you been? Man up, protect her. For once in your damn life, step up for someone else!" I shout at Rex.

"Fuck you. What the hell do you know about my history with Tessie?"

"Shut the fuck up, both of you. Is someone gonna claim Tessie today?" Tripp looks to me before he can finish his next sentence, the sentence where I know he will tell us all we can't do anything for her.

Before I can think about what the hell I am doing, I speak up, "I claim her. She's my ol' lady."

"You sure? I haven't called Roundman yet to see if there is something else we can do for her," Tripp asks.

"I know the rules to this world, the spoken and the unspoken. Ruthless isn't club owned. Tessie isn't claimed. We can't seek retribution when she's not ours on a fuckin' technicality. Don't call Roundman, just let Thorn know she's mine and it's on him to give us Shep."

"I know you got a lot on your plate, Shooter, but that doesn't dismiss your actions in here today. Disrespect of an officer won't be tolerated. Once we get Shep handled, we will revisit this. You got me?"

"I got you. Wouldn't change a damn thing, so dish out your punishment accordingly."

Well, I would change shit. I would beat the ever loving shit out of Rex if I could. My brothers would never allow it, though. No, I am lucky they let me get him into the wall.

Tripp was there at my house last night with Doll. He saw first-hand what Tessie looked like before Doll and Doc Kelly got her cleaned up. If he hadn't been there, I am certain I wouldn't have been allowed any leniency to get my hands on Rex.

There is an almost unnoticeable chin lift by Tripp to me, his eyes showing respect and understanding for what this is doing to me. Tripp is Catawba club prez; he knows my history. He knows it claws at my insides to watch a strong, beautiful woman be destroyed while I sit helplessly on the sidelines.

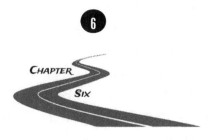

NOT DEFEATED

Waking to the discomfort of my aching body once again is a bold reminder of what I have endured. Today, however, is a new day.

It has been three days since my attack. Shooter has been great in opening his home to me. Doc Kelly has been in and out to redress my wounds and check me over. She left me with meds to help me sleep and for the pain. I am also on a course of antibiotics to fight infections given the wide range of my wounds. My face is still swollen, but I can at least open my eyes now.

I am getting by. My mom, being my mom, came by yesterday to see me. Doll stayed with me and held my hand as I shared the truth with my mom about my assault, the three of us crying together. She agrees we should tell Axel I was in an accident. Adult problems are just that—adult problems. I can't burden my little boy with what really happened.

Doll, being the boss lady she is, got all my shifts covered this week at both Brinkley's and Ruthless. Now I need to make some serious life decisions.

With the loss of my income this week, there is no way I will make my rent for next month, so step one is to pack my shit. Step two, settle back in at Mom's house. I knew this day was coming, but my situation warrants my making the transition a little sooner than I originally anticipated. Score another point for that bitch that happens to be life. I may get knocked down, but I will not be defeated.

Moving around slowly, I get up and dressed. Doll brought over a few of my things, so I begin to pack up what I have laying around Shooter's bedroom and bath. Until today, I haven't taken in much of my surroundings.

His room is large, although minimally filled. A king size bed on a frame with no headboard, no footboard and only one nightstand. Along the wall is one tall dresser covering the expansive space. His closet is one made for a couple, having individual sides. His side is full with jeans and T-shirts in different colors. A garment bag hangs full in the very back. His boots line up the floor in a straight row alongside two pairs of running shoes. The other side of the closet is completely empty, minus a large gun safe that is combination locked.

The bathroom is one designed with a woman in mind. The oversized tub has four jets that have been just what my aching body needed to relax while the sleeping pills kicked in. The double sinks allowed me to stay out of Shooter's way with my deodorant, toothbrush, and hair brush. His shower is enormous with two shower heads. If I combine his bathroom and closet, they are the size of my entire trailer.

The rest of Shooter's house is much of the same; very little furniture, nothing personal on display, and modern upgrades. His kitchen has maple colored cabinetry and fancy, stone countertops like you would see in one of those magazines at the end of the grocery store cash register. His living room has two built-in bookshelves on either side of a fireplace with a space for a television above it. The area is completely bare except for a TV and DVD player. The house has two smaller bedrooms that are practically empty.

Doc Kelly said fresh air would help me; as a result, I did venture out to the porch yesterday. Shooter has acreage. I'm not sure how much exactly, but he doesn't seem to have neighbors close by. A two car garage is separate from the house, the only other building visible. He has a nice yard, but no fence. The trees lining the property and driveway are the only view from all angles of the house. It is quiet here, which can be nice... or it can be haunting, depending on the moment.

Am I ready to face the outside world? Not really. I miss my son, though; therefore, I need to get going. Aware that the back and forth isn't good for him, I won't take him back to our old trailer. I will pack our stuff and get us settled in my old room at home where he sleeps when he stays with Mom.

"Goin' somewhere?" Shooter questions as he stands in the doorframe to his bedroom and sees my bag.

"Home," I answer honestly.

"So soon? You don't have to leave, Tessie." He stays where he is, watching me with concern in his features.

"I miss Axel. Thanks for all you've done."

I move to the bathroom to grab the few toiletries I have here. What should I say? Thanks for saving my life. I don't know for sure if the guy would have killed me, but I also don't know that he would have spared me, either. The last few moments of the altercation are little fuzzy. I don't remember Shooter coming in or how I got out of there exactly. I just remember hearing Shooter's voice.

As a thought hits me, I lean against the bathroom wall and slide down it to the floor.

Shooter is immediately standing at my side without touching me. "What's wrong, Tessie?"

"The guy... the guy... is he alive? Is he going to come after me again?" My body trembles as the fear once again consumes me.

"Baby, I don't know if he's alive. I shot him twice in the legs. I didn't want to risk you, so I only injured him enough to get you outta there."

Unable to stop the sobs, I sit there as tears fall down my face. Slowly, I watch Shooter squat down beside me. Then shaking thumbs reach out and wipe away my tears.

"He's not gonna come after you again. Not if he wants to live. Tessie, I wanted to wait to talk to you, but I guess now is as good a time as any."

I look at him in confusion. Talk to me about what?

He sits down on his bathroom floor beside me. I have noticed he goes out of his way to make sure I am not spooked or don't have to move. It is more than consideration, too. Shooter moves around me cautiously, like he would move heaven and earth to keep from scaring me.

"Tessie, I claimed you," he states, as if this is something that happens every single day.

"What do you mean *claimed me?*" I ask on a hiccup as my sobbing subsides.

"I made you my ol' lady."

His words don't register with me right away. "Why?" I ask since that's all I can seem to think.

"I know who attacked you, but being as it was another club, the only way to truly protect you was for someone to step up and claim you."

"And that someone was you?"

"Yeah, baby, it was me. You gotta know, it's just in name. After we handle the Ghosts, I'll let ya go. You obviously don't hafta stay here and be my real ol' lady. In public, you're mine so you gotta remember that. It's to protect you."

My mind runs a mile a minute. "Why do I have to be claimed? I don't understand."

"It's the way of my world. In order for the club to protect you and act on your behalf of what has happened, you have to be property of the club. You're a female and can't be a brother, so your way in is as an ol' lady."

"So anyone could've stepped up to protect me by claiming me?"

"Well, it usually doesn't work this way. Usually,

you're in a relationship with the woman, but we needed our name to cover you. This was the only way."

"No, no, I get that, Shooter. I'm sayin,' out of every single brother, any one of them could've stepped up, but you did?"

He stares at me in confusion. "I told you already. I did."

"Rex?" I whisper then watch his eyebrows rise in understanding.

He drops his head before answering me. "He wasn't at the sermon, but a decision had to be made quickly, so I stepped in. He couldn't do anything after it was done."

While relief washes over me because I have no business being Rex's ol' lady—in reality, I don't want to be an old lady at all—I can't help wondering why Shooter dropped his head and didn't face me and tell me. Is he afraid I would be disappointed Rex wasn't there?

With the history I share with Rex, it would crush me to know that, when I needed him most, he didn't step up for me. I find comfort in the fact that he wasn't there. At least that way I can hold on to some sort of hope that, even if we won't ever be together, he would do whatever was necessary to keep me safe. However, after all of this, there is no way in hell Rex and I will ever be anything more than friends. I want to pick up the pieces of my life and raise my son. Nothing more, nothing less.

SHOOTER

I t has been one month since my world was turned on its axis yet again. One month ago, Tessie was harmed. She is healing now, but my house feels empty without her. The day after I claimed her, she moved home with her mom. Her aunt and I helped her pack.

Yeah, I lied to her about Rex. One day, I will clear it up; however, with everything she has already been through, I didn't want to add to her disappointments. It is clear things with her and Rex are over.

The guys have all gotten the word out about Tessie being my ol' lady. Even though it isn't real, I feel connected to her. I want her protected. While my instincts scream to go get her and drag her home with me, I know inside I am no good for her. Inside, I know she can't really be mine. I am worried about her, but I don't want to push.

With her mom keeping me updated, I know Tessie hasn't checked her bank account and things are rough. She doesn't know the club and I deposited more than enough money to cover her bills and living expenses. Still, I feel better having her at home with her mom instead of the trailer.

Bob said he has called her and keeps up with her, but she hasn't returned to Ruthless for work. She knows she has a job there whenever she feels ready to return, though. Bob is pretty torn up about what happened and agreed to sell ten percent of the bar to the Hellions, so it is off limits to outsiders now. He also promised never to leave anyone to close up alone again. It's too little, too late as far as I'm concerned.

A patched brother will now be there at closing every night. Even if Tessie doesn't come back, at least we know Corinne and now, Pamela will be safe. Bob took Pamela on to replace Tessie until she decides if she will return or not.

Tessie hasn't returned to Brinkley's yet, either, but Corinne says she plans to work there next week. I am glad to see her trying to get back to normal, whatever that may be.

Her mom says she hasn't been eating much or sleeping well. Maybe, if she gets back to work, things will settle in her mind and she will take better care of herself.

Stepping into the cave for sermon, I'm on edge. Tripp has called today's meeting to update us on the Ghosts. The bastards have been smart, staying out of the Carolinas.

After the call to order, Tripp wastes no time in delivering the news.

"Thorn says Shep has gone underground. He doesn't have contact with him at the moment."

"Underground? Fuck that. He's goin' *in* the ground. What kind of operation is Thorn runnin' that he can't keep track of his boys?" I ask.

"Thorn obviously has his plate full—" Tripp starts, but I wade in before he can continue.

"It's about to get a lot fuller. My ol' lady was attacked by one of his crew. If he can't deliver Shep to us, then his whole club can suffer the consequences for one man's actions for all I care." It surprises even me how easily the words ol' lady roll off my tongue.

"You're talkin' war," Rex says, watching me, "for a piece of pussy you've never even had." The cocky bastard smiles sardonically at me. "You really think the club should risk all of us for her?"

When Head Case puts a firm hand on my shoulder to hold me in place it does nothing to stop me from running my mouth.

"What a true piece of shit you are. How's she not worth it? If it were Doll, hands down we'd all be voting it to take them all out." Looking at the man who is trying to remind me to stay put as his hand is still on my shoulder, I make my point to Head Case. "If this were Doc Kelly, would there be a question of how the vote would go? Rex has fucked her over enough through the years, and none of us touched her because of him. This whole thing would've never happened to her if he'd stepped up for her a long time ago, or if he had been man enough to let her go. Now, I sit here with her, knowing she's my ol' lady, and I have to wonder if my brothers are gonna go to bat for my woman. That's some real brotherhood we're showin' here."

"Enough," Tripp states, eyes on Rex. "I've given Thorn seventy-two hours to deliver Shep to us. If he doesn't, we need to vote on it. Are we goin' to war with the Ghosts for the attack on Tessie? They came to our bar—owned or not, people know—and they hurt one of our own."

Rex says nothing and his face gives away nothing.

Tripp continues, "We vote. If Shep isn't handed over in the next three days, we go to war with the Desert Ghosts. Those in agreement, aye; those not, disagree."

One by one, the brothers are asked. Their votes count, don't get me wrong, but it is the officer's table I want to see. More importantly, my VP; where does he stand? As the votes come in, so far, all but three agree to the stipulation of war if Shep isn't turned over. The room is all in agreement by majority, the last two votes aren't necessary; however, as Prez and VP, they still announce their decisions.

While Tripp looks to Rex as it is his turn to cast a vote, the bastard glances at me and winks. If he disagrees, I am going to kill him with my bare hands. After all the years Tessie has remained on the back-burner for him, he wouldn't choose not go to bat for her, would he?

"Aye. That bastard touched the wrong one. They hand him over, or I'll go after every single one of them, one by mother fuckin' one."

Rex's response shocks me, making me release the breath I was holding. He was fucking with me this whole time. He may not claim her, but he will go to war for her. I still hate the bastard because he could have and should have stayed to make sure she wasn't alone. All of this could have been prevented.

"Aye," Tripp states. "If Thorn doesn't comply, war it will be." The gavel slams down and the sermon is dismissed.

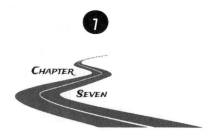

ADJUSTING... OR NOT

T he visible wounds have healed for the most part. I will forever carry a scar across my forehead and the bump on my nose. I am managing to work at Brinkley's a few days a week now. Moreover, thanks to the additional funds in my bank account, I have stayed afloat without working like I was before. Granted, I think, when the club, Shooter, or whomever made the deposit in my account, they were expecting me to pay rent with it. However, since I moved out of my trailer, I don't have the expense; as a result, I have been able to carry the money further. The landlord was nice about my departure. She said she would leave the place empty for me for a few months to get back on my feet. I wish she wouldn't hold it. It is more than the money, though; I just didn't bother telling her that. Pride gets the best of us all. I don't want to swallow mine and tell her that I won't be moving out of my mom's again.

Shooter stops in to check on me at work, but has otherwise kept his distance over the last few weeks. Strangely enough, I find that I miss him. In this entire ordeal, he has not once pushed me.

Doll has tried to get me back to Ruthless. According to her, Bob, and Corinne, Ruthless is Hellion owned now, so I am safe to return.

Safe.

Do they not understand? I thought I was safe before.

Shep, the name I have since learned, had been in Ruthless multiple times over the last few months, and not once did I think he would attack me. Sure, he was always filthy. He always looked disheveled with greasy hair and in need of a shave, smelling like the road and cigarettes. He liked his Jack straight and chain smoked with no regard to your own health when he blew his secondhand smoke in your face. He was an asshole, but ninety percent of the guys I deal with are, including the Hellions.

It's the nature of the beast, as some would say. I work in a testosterone filled environment where they all swing their dicks around to show who is in charge at least once a night. These aren't pretty boys in suits. No, I have always been surrounded by the chaos and reckless abandon of bikers. Up until my attack, I never gave it a second thought. I have a kid to feed, clothes to put on his back, and a roof to keep over his head. I didn't have time to think about what could happen. My mistake. I allowed myself to become comfortable.

Mercy, she is a bitch and fails to shine down on me. With everything I have dealt with in my life, you would think by now I would know better. I should find the bad in every situation and know it will happen to me at some point. I had my own place, a little money in the bank (certainly not a lot, but I knew my rent would be paid), and Axel and I were doing well. Therefore, I should have expected something to come along and knock me on my ass.

A knock at the door brings me back to this moment. My mom is resting in her room and Axel is at school. I make my way to the door, hoping my mom stays asleep. I have been keeping her up lately and she could use the rest.

Looking through the peephole, my breath catches in

my chest. Shooter stands on the other side, waiting. Realistically, seeing him shouldn't bother me. It does, however. He has truly seen me at my worst. How do I handle him? How does he handle me?

Taking a deep breath, I open the door to him. Plastering on the best smile I can, I drink in the man in front of me. He's not overly built, but he is fit, there is no denying it. Shooter has no visible tattoos, which makes me curious since every single one of the Hellions have multiple tattoos.

My mind wanders, thinking back to all the times he has come to the bar. He is always alone. Unlike Rex, Tripp, before Doll, or any of the other guys, Shooter is not one to hook up with the barflies, at least not publicly.

"You gonna let me in?" he questions, taking me away from my thoughts.

"Ummm… Why are you here?"

"I came to check on you."

Stepping back, I gesture with my hand for him to come inside. Somehow, having him near sends my body into overdrive. My heart races, but not in fear. No, Shooter is the one person who calms me when the negative overruns my brain. Regardless, I can't allow myself to become used to him. I can't depend on him or anyone, for that matter; therefore, I need to keep him at a distance.

He follows me into the living room. It is a small space where Mom's old, brown couches have seen better days. Axel has left his artistic marks all over them. We don't have a coffee table anymore. My childhood dog, Fescue, knocked into it, breaking it, and Mom never replaced it. The two accent tables are covered in doilies and soft lamps. The television is not very big in screen size, but it is old so the box is huge to move around. It sits on the same stand it has been on for the last fifteen years. Mom's place is bigger than my trailer; yet not by much. It certainly isn't adorned with life's finer things.

Having Shooter here agitates me a little bit. I have never cared what anyone thought before, but there is something about him that makes me not want him to see this broken down side of me. No hiding it now, though; he is here and apparently not in a hurry to leave.

"See for yourself." I wave my hands. "I'm here."

"How ya holdin' up, Tessie? Be straight with me."

"I'm holdin' up, Shooter. There's nothing more I can say. I'm adjusting," I answer, not really sure where he is going with this.

"Or not. You sleepin' okay?"

"Yeah."

He reaches his hand up to my face, his thumb gently coming down to trace the bags under my left eye. I flinch involuntarily at the contact before closing my eyes and taking a deep breath. It's just Shooter.

He immediately withdraws, but watches me closely.

"Tessie, you don't look like you're sleepin', baby."

"I'm doin' the best I can."

"Your mom, she's worried. I know you're doin' the best you can, but it's more than you. Tell me, Tessie, what can I do to help you?" Shooter asks with such a pull in his tone I can't deny that he is hurting for me.

"Time heals all wounds, or so they say," I answer kindly.

"Baby, this is killing me. It's killin' all of us to know we can't help you. Stay with me."

"What?" I ask, not hiding my shock at his request.

"Stay at my place. I can help with your mom and Axel. You won't have to feel alone. I know you're aware we got men watchin' this place, but your mom called me. She thinks you might do better out of here. I know you don't want to leave her or Axel, but my place is plenty big. Stay with me. All of you, come stay with me."

"Shooter, have you thought this through?" I question, knowing I don't need to think a damn thing through. Shooter may have the best intentions in the world to help me; however, he doesn't know my story. If he did, he wouldn't be opening his home to me, nor would any of his brothers.

"To be honest, no, Tessie, I haven't. What I do know is you are going through the motions, but you aren't healing. I'll do whatever it takes to help you heal, baby."

"Stayin' at your place won't heal me. Thanks for your kindness, but I just need some time." At my refusal, I gesture for us to make our way back to the door.

"You want me to leave?" Shooter asks, not one to beat around the bush.

"Yeah, I think you should go. Nothin' personal, Shooter, but you can't heal me... no one can." My last few words come out in a whisper as I drop my head in defeat.

"This is killin' me," I hear him mutter as he exits the house.

Closing the door behind him, I lean against it, letting my mind run with how to pick up the pieces of my life. The rumble of his bike cranking causes my heart to skip a beat. I listen as the steady tick of the engine becomes a soothing rhythm as he idles in my driveway. My thoughts slow, and I feel like I can focus on my next steps when I finally hear him pull away. Then there's the click as he changes gears, the rev of the throttle as he drives off, and in the distance, the drop as he shifts gears, speeding away to face the outside world.

SHOOTER

S ermon has been called again. Given my role within the club has never involved transports, I am learning more about that side of our business on the fly. There are two sides to the transportation company. The side that does hauling and moving like most of the truckers running the roads. Then there is the side that gets into business with the likes of the Desert Ghosts. Apparently, my motorcycle club has been offering protection for the Ghosts' shipments through the Carolinas. We have also arranged some trades with the reservation and handled protection for the once affiliated club. Now I know why the Ghosts have been in and out so much recently, following up on business.

We all gather in, and Tripp quickly calls the meeting to open.

"Shooter, first order, you need to move Tessie, her

boy, and her mom in with you within the week. Roundman secured information for us on some Ghosts' shipments. We need every spare man we got out on the run. We also don't need any distractions for us back home. You handle keeping Tessie and her family safe. We will handle stirring things up for Thorn and crew."

"Tripp, this isn't a normal relationship. She may not want to move in with me so easily," I inform my club Prez as I remember four days ago when Tessie looked worn slam out yet still refused help.

"I get that, but make her see. This is for the club as a whole now. We gave Thorn three days to cough up Shep. He didn't. My word is we are goin' to war. Unlike Thorn, I have my shit together, and we're goin' after 'em with everything we've got. Handle your woman," Tripp commands, like this would be as simple as explaining it to Doll.

"Fuck! She's been through enough. Now I gotta rip her from her home? Hell, she doesn't even want me around."

"Move in with her, then. Either way, I gotta pull the guard off Tessie and onto the road. We got eyes on Doll, Doc Kelley, and the other ol' ladies, but I don't wanna put just anyone inside the house with her outta respect for what she went through. It has to be you"—he looks at me then turns his gaze to his cousin and VP— "or I leave Rex behind and he steps in. Which way do you want it, Shooter? You claimed her, now the question is… you gonna step up?" Tripp throws my own words in my face.

Rex grins at me. "I'll take real good care of her, too, man."

As something inside me snaps, Head Case senses it and grabs me when I start to lunge at Rex.

"Fuck off, Rex. She's mine; I'll handle it."

Piece of shit, son of a bitch. How can he act like this about Tessie? She is not a barfly. I don't know how far back they go, but those two share a history that is more than either have let on to, yet the fucker is goading me into beating his ass over her.

"Make it happen, Shooter," Tripp orders, knowing he's pushed me over the edge with Rex.

"Affirmative," I agree, still uncertain as to how I am going to tackle the newest Tessie dilemma.

CHAPTER EIGHT

TERRORS

"Wouldn't serve me earlier, bitch, but you'll serve me now." I hear him.

Whiskey... cigarettes... I smell him. He is on me. The weight pressing against me. His weight. His fingers... Oh, God, his fingers... This can't be happening.

"Noooooooo!" I scream out into the night.

Startled, I wake up, drenched in a cold sweat and

tangled in my sheets. Looking around, I see I am in my childhood bedroom. Lavender walls still surround me along with my white lace curtains and white furniture that haven't changed since I was twelve or so. My eyes adjust to the darkness as I work to settle my breathing. Scanning my darkened space, I stop when I lock eyes on the man in my doorway.

"Shooter," I whisper.

This can't be real. No way, no how is he here in the middle of the night, standing in my doorway, wearing nothing other than some low slung sweatpants. No way, no how can my heart rate speed up in lust for the sculpted man who is mostly a mystery to me. After everything I have been through, why is my body betraying me now? It is Shooter, that's why. I feel safe with him.

God, I am losing my mind. I pat the bedding around me, trying to gather my bearings. The shadow of Shooter isn't really here; therefore, he can't be moving over to my bed... can he?

"No, no, no," I whisper into the air around me.

"Calm down, baby."

Somebody call Doc Kelly because I am seriously losing my ever loving mind. There is no way Shooter is here, talking to me.

I push back my now wet hair from sweating during my nightmare. Then, taking a deep breath, I close my eyes. *Get it together, Tessie.* I blow out my breath and open my eyes. Shooter is now sitting with one leg hanging off my bed, watching me.

"Breathe, baby. Inhale," he gently commands. "Exhale."

These much needed simple reminders take the edge off the rising fear inside me. Doing as instructed, I find myself settling down, the panic subsiding. How does this man calm me?

"Shooter, why are you here?"

"Some things are changing, and I need to be here for a little while. I'll sleep on the couch. You won't notice me," Shooter answers, watching me.

My breathing accelerates as my palms get clammy. Panic fills me once again, but for a totally different reason as I think about him being here in my home. Oh, God, what am I going to do?

"Tessie, you need to sleep."

"No, Shooter, I need to shower, and you need to go home. I'll make do. I always find a way."

"It's not that simple."

"Look, I'm sorry to inconvenience you with being here, even though I didn't ask you to come, I might add. I'm also sorry I woke you up, but you need to go home," I state, hoping like hell he leaves.

"Club orders, baby. Either I stay here, or you, your

boy, and your mom all have to stay with me. Not negotiable."

"I'm not part of the club, so the Hellions' orders are irrelevant to me."

He leans in close to me, his hands on either side of me as he comes in nose to nose with me. Our breathing comes and goes together while we both fight to maintain our composure.

"Baby, the minute I claimed you, the club owned you." His face changes into an unreadable emotion. "Is there another brother you'd rather have? Hmmm...?" His agitation with me is no longer held back.

"Shooter, this isn't about Rex." Pausing, I decide to be as honest as I have ever been with anyone about Drexel "Rex" Crews. "Well, it is, but not like you think." There, I admitted it. Everything with me is tied to Rex, only no one knows it.

He backs away from me only slightly. "So tell me." He says it so simply. If only it was that easy.

At first, keeping quiet wasn't a problem. As time passes, though, it is no longer about keeping my secret. Now, I have to worry about the repercussions of my once clear decision. My mind spins further. I need space.

"Go home, Shooter," I command as I push up and off the bed, brushing him off as I get up.

Avoiding the biker in my room, I grab some clothes

and go down the hall to take a shower. Hopefully, by the time I get out, he will be gone and this will be a nightmare.

The water running over me does nothing to calm my emotions. As I squirt some dollar store body wash on my loofa, I begin to lather and wash my body. Once again, I am quickly lost to my thoughts, to my nightmares. I watch the soap against my skin, but I can't get clean. Turning the hot water on high and the cold completely off, I allow the liquid to scald my skin. Still not feeling clean, I scrub harder with my loofa; however, it is not enough.

I pull at my roots as I wash my hair. I want it to go away. I want to go back in time and call in sick that night. Hell, I don't want to be with Rex, but if I would have given in to him that night, *it* wouldn't have happened. If I had never gotten involved with Rex in the first place, I wouldn't be working at Ruthless in the first place. Shoulda, coulda, woulda. It is a constant battle in my mind. Oh, the things I would change. Hindsight is twenty-twenty, as they say.

Feeling like I may pass out from the heat, I rinse and get out of the shower. Drying off, I can only pat my now raw skin.

Making a quick walk through the house, I don't find Shooter on the couch or anywhere. I guess he took me at my word.

Lying down, I toss and turn the same as I do every night. The bed is hard and unmoving, much like that wall. The unforgiving wall that aided in holding me immobile that night.

Exhaustion is consuming me because I haven't slept a full night since the incident. I am not awake, but I am not in a dreamland of comfortable slumber. I twist as I find myself tangled and trapped in my own bed.

Strong arms scoop me up. How? I am sleeping, yet I feel him with me now. Shooter. That night, Shep was about to enter me. Shooter came, though. He carried me out. He kept me safe.

"I've been there, Tessie," Shooter's voice whispers in my ear, "where the silence is deafening. Where everything is so dark on the inside, the light of day won't break through as you go through the motions. When the darkness falls and your mind takes your body back to the place where it all falls apart."

My limbs feel heavy as I relax into his hold. He is saving me in my dreams even. My eyelids are far too heavy to lift as I drift further into sleep.

"Don't let the black engulf you, baby. Fight it, Tessie. Fight it for Axel."

The bed beneath me feels softer now, inviting almost.

Whispered words fill my mind.

"Fight it, baby. Fight for peace. Fight to have your

life back. Fight back the darkness. Fight it for your mom."

Drifting deeper into sleep, I hear Shooter whisper one more time. "Hell, baby, fight it for me. Fight it for what could be."

SHOOTER

S leep will be left to the angels tonight. A call from
Tessie's mom, Claire, brought me over this
evening. My plan was to talk to Tessie tomorrow about
our living arrangements, only Claire is worried about
her daughter. She is also worried about all of their
safety. Although we have someone on guard, the rota-
tion of men she doesn't know is stressing Claire out.
With her illness, stress is a trigger for flare ups, and she
certainly has enough stress without the addition of
strangers coming and going. The reality is, I am a
stranger to her, as well, but she knows some of what
happened and apparently feels like I am a family friend
or at least a guardian. She called to ask me to stay over
because Tessie seems to be having issues with
nightmares.

The couch was the only available space for me to

sleep other than the floor. I had barely closed my eyes when Tessie's scream startled me. Sure, she told me to leave. The hell if I plan to do that, though, especially after seeing for myself that Claire is right. The physical signs of depression are there: weight loss, withdrawing, irritability, and many more I am sure I could pinpoint if I spent more time with Tessie. No, I am not going home.

Sorry, baby, but I am locking down and staying now. Not just on Tripp's order, but for your own well-being, Tessie.

Hiding in the shadows isn't hard when she gets out of the shower. Watching her lie down and not find peace is a torture like nothing I have faced before. She is hurting, and I am helpless to bring her peace.

Then something in me comes alive, some pull that I long ago shut down snaps back. Involuntarily, I find myself needing to comfort her.

When she doesn't fight me as I climb in her bed and hold her, I don't know what to think. Following my instincts, I talk her down from the panic she was building up just moments ago. She is not fully awake, yet not in a deep sleep, either; she is drifting in a way.

Night terrors—I have been there. You feel like you are awake and stuck in some horrific moment. You move and fight out against an invisible assailant. The world you are in is not your own, but one vividly recreated in your mind. Your bed is suddenly a person, a wall, or a cage containing you. Lashing out, you struggle, waging war in your mind against yourself. Muscles exerted, calories burned, sweat pours from your body as your imagination works in overdrive. Your pulse quickens, your breathing labors, and you continue to fight in vain until, hopefully, you wake up. Hopefully, something pulls you slowly out of the dream and into the reality. And, more importantly, this all occurs before you hurt yourself or someone else.

Whispering softly to her, I follow my instincts to let her know she is not alone. She is resting on me as I lay on my back before she shifts to cover my chest. Evening out my breathing to match hers, I lie in the quiet of the dark, trying to push down the many emotions coursing through me.

There is a connection I have to her, one I can't begin to understand.

Tessie is a beautiful woman. She has a quiet strength, carrying herself with grace and humility. She is everything I have never had in a woman, and I have had my fair share of barflies since Tracie.

Tracie. People say she is my angel now, watching over me. Ha! That is so far from the truth even the devil himself wouldn't tell that lie. She died hating me, hating everything I stood for, everything I had done. She is no angel of mine. She is the sins of my past all bundled into my lifelong nightmare; everything I wanted for my future taken from me at her blood covered hands.

It is my fault. We got together much too young. She was a down home girl that wanted the regular life. To her, our future was me turning wrenches in her dad's garage for life. I, being the young guy, wanted the adrenaline pumping, push my body beyond its limits life of a soldier.

We were together all four years of high school. After graduation, I left for boot camp, and then it was off to tech school for my MOS (Military Occupational Specialty). Not long after that, it was selection for SF (Special Forces) teams. She went through the motions, but she wasn't happy, nagging me constantly about being away.

I tried to break up with her because my career was important to me. However, she was having none of that. I made it through selection and training and earned my green beret. Whereas my parents were proud to see their son become one of the elite, my girlfriend was miserable. I almost proposed thinking the commitment might help her adjust…only I didn't. Then it was too late.

I was stationed in Fort Bragg, North Carolina and assigned to my team. Multiple trainings and deployments only strengthened my bond with my Army brothers, while those same separations from Tracie only furthered our divide. I was trained to withstand torture. I was trained to not carry ties to back home with me. I was trained to shut out everything around me except the mission at hand.

I was not trained to handle the emotions of a woman. I was not trained in how to support someone who wouldn't support me. I was not equipped to see the signs of depression in my girlfriend.

My teammates, yes, I knew those boys better than my own damn family. Lock, for instance. When he would think of his sister Laura back home, his left jaw would twitch. Any other time, he would have a face of stone on a mission. Let him have idle time to think of his little sister and the twitch would start with a steady, even pace as his jaw pulsed, matching the slow rate of our hearts in stealth mode.

Bowie, he was hard. His life back home was far from easy. He grew up in a motorcycle club. His dad, being club prez to the Savage Outlaws, ultimately left him to raise himself. Bowie joined the Army, needing the discipline to tame his reckless abandon, and he needed the escape for a bit. Not much could faze him after being raised in his lifestyle. Fatigue, on the other hand... When Bowie would get worn down, he would start running his hands through his short hair. It seemed to wake him up for a bit. Other than that, Bowie was unreadable. Eyes of steel, giving nothing away; face of a hard-working man with no fear; and hands that never shook and never faltered. After a few tours, the life of a soldier wears on you. Not long after my discharge, he returned to his hometown and club life.

Hammer, who got his name for having an iron fist, would fidget with his hands when annoyed. The more worked up he would get, the more he twisted his hands or twiddled his thumbs, unable to keep them still.

Spending so much time with those guys, I couldn't help studying them. Sometimes life and death could depend on being able to read the look in your brother's eye. Non-verbal communication can sometimes speak volumes without one sound being shared.

If only I had paid more attention to Tracie. I could have seen the internal battle she was facing. Tunnel vision for my career, my wants, and my needs all clouded my view, making me unable to see how everything I did was affecting her.

Looking down at Tessie, I watch as she continues to breathe softly on my chest.

How can I know the individual ticks of my Army brothers yet not see the slow deterioration of the woman I had claimed to love? Tracie was open with her hatred of my job. However, rather than listen and pay attention to her body language, I chalked it up to her being a needy bitch.

I should have paid attention. I should have been more supportive. I should have been more understanding. Compromise, something that never once crossed my mind before, but is now my biggest regret. I forced my choices on her. It was take me as I am or not at all. I never sought out a way to meet her in the middle on anything.

Allowing my mind to go back through my past regrets, I watch as Tessie seems to be at peace in my arms. She fits somehow. This is a foreign feeling to me.

Whispering into the night, I muse, "Oh, baby, what are you doing to me? You are stirring up too much of my past. I wasn't man enough to save Tracie; I don't know that I'm man enough to save you."

As if she heard me, Tessie snuggles in closer, holding my waist tighter as she nestles her face against my chest once more.

"Mercy, shine down on her. Give her peace, if for just one night," I whisper once more as I close my eyes, knowing I won't really get any sleep.

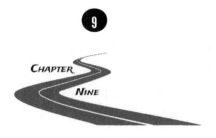

CHAPTER NINE

TRUTH

Warm. I feel warm. Safe.

Arms envelope me, providing comfort and a security I have never felt before. I don't want to get up. For the first time, I want to stay asleep. For once, I am feeling somewhat rested.

Wait. Arms? Who is with me?

Breathing deeply, I don't even open my eyes. Shooter.

What the hell am I going to do?

Cracking one eye open, I try to ignore the masculine perfection under me and look at the clock on my dresser. Eight twelve in the morning. Shit! I am so fucking screwed right now. Axel is late for school. More than that, he will be coming in my room any minute, I am sure of it. My secret is no longer safe.

"I know you're awake, baby," Shooter says without moving under me. His arms are still casually slung over me like we sleep together all the time.

Refusing to answer him, I only close my eyes and blow out my breath.

"I don't mind spending the day like this if that's what you want," he adds while gently rubbing my back.

"What are you doing here?" I ask without bothering to get off him just yet.

"Some things have changed with the club. I need to be here."

"No, you don't," I argue.

Shooter shifts under me, moving to sit up against the headboard, easily moving me with him. My full size bed gives me little room to escape him. His hold is gentle yet firm and not something I altogether want to get out of.

"Baby, it's time we have a talk about club life. What has Rex told you about women and the Hellions?"

At the mention of my ex-fling, I flinch. Rex, yeah,

he is not the person I want to talk about before I have had even a drop of coffee.

"Not a damn thing. Truth be told—" I am cut off by Shooter.

"Nothing? He shared nothing with you? Not even for your own safety?" I feel Shooter getting tense under me.

Having someone so protective of me is a new experience.

"I don't want to know, Shooter," I tell him calmly, knowing he is full of unease at my lack of knowledge.

"There are things you can't know, Tessie. Things you will never know. It's just club business."

"Again, Shooter," I interject, "I don't want to know."

"Want is irrelevant at this point in our relationship. You are now in a situation of need to know, baby. I claimed you; do you understand that?"

"Yeah, I get it. I'm club property. I'm a representation of the Hellions and a direct representation of you. I fall under the halo of Hellion protection as your ol' lady. I have no rights, no information, and no opinion of my own. I show up where I'm told as an arm piece to do as I'm told and ride where I'm told. I'm not to make a scene or disrespect you or any one of your brothers. If we were lovers, I would be expected to fuck you when you wanted to fuck, how you wanted to fuck, and however you wanted to fuck. I, however, would have no say whatsoever in whom you chose to fuck other than me. Furthermore, I would not be allowed to fuck anyone else since you cavemen don't like to share while we women have to watch you get off by someone else, should you choose. Yup, Shooter, I got it. I know my damn place." My tone is not sharp, my voice never rising, as I lay it out there for him calmly. I am not one for the dramatics or yelling. It is what it is. If there is a shit hand to be dealt, I know it will be placed in front of me. As such, there's no need to cause a ruckus.

"Baby, who the fuck have you been talkin' to? Do you really think for one second that's how it is?"

"Shooter, I work at Ruthless. The barflies talk. Hell, your brothers get drunk and bitch constantly about their ol' ladies not walking the line."

"Baby, come on, you have to know better than to believe a bunch of whores and a bunch of drunken ramblings."

Leaning away from his chest, I look him in the eye without saying a word. Yes, I believe it. I have heard it enough times and from enough different sources. There is truth to what I've said.

"Baby, do you think for one second Doll would let Tripp step out on her or to not allow her an opinion on subjects that aren't club business? Hell, does Doll strike you as any man's arm piece?" he questions, making a valid point.

"Well, Doll and Tripp, that's different." Doll is the exception to every rule in my mind.

"And we aren't different? Cuz, baby, you aren't fuckin' me, and you're my ol' lady, and I'm not fuckin' anyone else."

"Shooter, we aren't in a real relationship. This is just temporary."

"Baby, this is for as long as it lasts, whatever may come, whatever may happen. I will share with you what I can, but beyond that, I can't. You can ask me questions, though I can't promise I will always answer them. You are right in that you are a representation of the Hellions and of me. You have rights, freedoms, and you have an opinion, one that means something to me. I won't fuck around on you. I won't disrespect you."

"Do you wanna fuck me?" I ask with trepidation evident in my voice.

Do I really want to know the answer to that question? I am still a woman, and one day I hope to move past what has happened to me. However, the thought of having sex terrifies me; there is no way I am anywhere near ready right now.

"Baby, I don't think you are ready to go there, even in conversation," Shooter responds, taking away my worries over him answering.

"I don't know what we're doing here," I state honestly. "Hell, I don't know what I'm doing with myself, much less adding you to the mix."

"I don't know what we're doing, either. So we'll figure it out together. First, you need to understand it's for the best if I stay here with you."

"No!" No way, no how. He cannot stay here. I am living on a prayer at the moment that I can nonchalantly hurry this conversation along to get Shooter gone long before Axel wakes up.

"Not negotiable. Second, you are my woman, for now. No disrespect to you will be given and none of the bullshit will be taken should you try to pull some. I've never seen you once act out with Rex, but I don't know what went on behind closed doors, either. I'm warning you once, I don't tolerate the dramatics. I'm an adult, you're an adult, and we treat each other like damn adults."

"Stop. This isn't happening," I try to interrupt him.

"Already happened baby. Look Tessie, I don't know you that well yet, and you don't know me. But we are in this situation together, so let's sort some shit early."

I nod silently just wanting to get this over with as he continues.

"Something about me you need to know. I have a very low tolerance for repeating myself. I'm done telling you what this is. I'm done telling you about the arrangements. You're my ol' lady, and I'm your man for as long as it lasts. I'm moving in. We'll both have to adjust to being so independent and now being together, but we will. We have to."

"Shooter, did you know all this when you claimed me?" For a second, I really want to know more about how this man's head ticks.

The pitter patter of little feet down the hall shakes me back into the moment. My world is crashing down around me as every second passes and every step that brings my son closer to my room.

SHOOTER

S hit! No fucking way. The little boy walking over to the bed is the spitting image of Rex. From the dirty blonde hair to his eyes to the strong jaw line and even the way the little guy carries himself, this is Rex's son.

Tessie tenses beside me, dropping her hand to my waist and her head to my chest as if she is holding me in place and hiding her face from me at the same time. With her palm clammy against my abdominal muscles, I flex involuntarily as my pulse races and my thoughts run together. The whole time, Tessie shudders on top of me, yet remains silently in place.

The mini Crews glares at me in defense of his mother as he approaches my side of the bed. He is in no way backing down from me or what he obviously considers his place.

Temper, temper, little shit-head.

"What the hell, Tessie?" I question, unable to form any other words.

"Momma says hell is a bad word; you shouldn't say it," the little fucker chastises.

"Axel, you need to go eat breakfast. Something easy, baby. We're running late," Tessie instructs her son.

"Be nice to my momma," Axel declares before leaving the room.

Is my anger that apparent? At least one of the Crews men is willing to step up, no matter the fight ahead for their woman.

Rex, the motherfucker, sure ain't nice to your momma, boy.

"Shooter," Tessie whispers beside me.

"You have some explaining to do—" Interrupting, she pushes off me, trying to get away from me and this conversation.

When I reach out and grab her arm, squeezing gently she stills, yet doesn't flinch or pull away. I am pissed, yes, but I would never hurt her.

She turns her head to meet my stare, her eyes filling with unshed tears.

"Like right fuckin' now, Tessie. I need to know."

Sighing, she says, "Stay put. Let me get him to school, then I promise to talk to you when I get back."

"Negative. *We* will take Axel to school. When *we*

come home, *you* will tell me everything. But, most importantly, you will tell me the truth, the whole truth."

Tessie tucks her hair behind her ears, her nervous habit. She does it when the guys at the bar hit on her and she is uncomfortable. It is something I have noticed and found attractive about her in the past. In this moment, it makes me on edge.

Please, Tessie, be honest with me. I can't handle being lied to, not when I have put so much on the line for you.

For a brief moment, anger and sadness flash across her features before she tucks the emotions away in true Tessie fashion. The slight blink of her eyes gives her away, although only for a moment. Anyone who isn't around Tessie regularly would probably look at her right now and say she is extremely strong and handling this well. However, I can see beyond the strong face, the hidden emotions, and into the shattered soul of the woman before me.

"Shooter, I need to get Axel to school without him questioning more of his life than he already is right now. He knows something is going on with me - more than I don't feel good. He knows we moved out of our trailer to move home with his Gigi. He's had enough on his plate for the last few months, so don't add to it in front of my son. When we get home, I will talk with you about him and answer the questions I see written all over your face."

"With complete, candid honesty?"

"Look, I know you don't have to help me. I appreciate everything you've done, really. Let's get one thing straight right now, though," she begins without raising her voice, but rather taking a sharp tone with me that reminds me of my own mother when I would get in trouble as a child. "Axel is my number one priority. I don't give a shit what you think of me, what your club thinks of me, or what anyone thinks of me. That boy is mine. He's been mine and only mine since the day he was conceived. I will answer anything you ask, openly and honestly, as long as you remember not to cross the line of my son's well-being. I may not have made all the right decisions, but I've done the best I could with the circumstances."

"Never said you didn't, Tessie."

"No, but I see the judgment written all over your face."

"Point taken. We will talk when we get home." Raising my hands in defeat, I decide to be her friend in this moment until I know what is going on here.

Aware she needs space from me, I get up from the bed and make my way out to the living room where I dropped my duffel bag the night before.

I have hundreds of questions running through my

mind. Tessie is a good mom; no one would question that. Why is she so defensive? Why isn't Rex around? Does he even know?

Rage builds inside me. Did that piece of shit motherfucker turn his back on them? I know he is a selfish prick, but certainly he wouldn't abandon his own kid. He wouldn't leave them to struggle financially while he is doing okay for himself, would he? I want to beat the shit out of my brother in this very moment. Even if he doesn't know—fuck that... how can he not know? They have been fucking for years. I know he has been to Tessie's house.

Inhaling deeply, I blow out my breath harshly in an attempt to calm myself. How can Tessie allow such disrespect? What makes Rex being around without being a dad okay in her book?

The feel of little eyes watching me has me turning around after pulling my shirt over my head. Axel is staring at me with a firm face for a six- or seven-year-old, little boy.

"Why are you here, Mister?" he boldly questions me.

Damn, the kid's got balls of steel.

"I'm a friend of your mom's."

"Momma don't have friends. She don't need friends. She's got me and Gigi. That's all she needs. You can leave and don't look back." Without waiting for me to reply, he turns and walks out of the living room.

I make my way to the bathroom to change my pants and wash up before taking the little hellion to school. When he comes around the corner with his blonde locks hidden under a baseball hat, I realize how Tessie has gotten him past the brothers we have had watching her.

The car ride is made in silence. While I wait for Tessie to return from signing Axel in, I try to get my emotions in check. Ultimately, this isn't my business, or it *wasn't* my business. Dammit, the lines are completely blurred with her. The longer she takes, the more I start looking around the building for exit points. Certainly she wouldn't run from me over this, right?

Just as I am about to get out of the car to go search for her, she climbs in the passenger seat of the Challenger.

"Sorry. He was late, so I had to sign him in at the actual office and explain his tardy."

"What the fuck is there to explain? You're his damn mom and you brought him to school. It ain't nobody's business why he's late," I say as my agitation grows once again.

"School policy," Tessie replies calmly.

Rather than start what I know will be an intense conversation in the car, I take Tessie back to my house. Pulling up, her surprise at our destination is evident.

"Why are we here?" she asks as I unlock the front door and let us in.

"I need to get shit for your house, and we need to talk, but I don't want your mom to overhear. She worries about you; you know?"

Anger flashes in her face before she pushes it back down. "Don't you get all righteous on me like you know about my life! Yes, Shooter, I am well fuckin' aware of my mom and her worries."

"Sit your ass down on the couch. Let me get my shit together, and then we're gonna talk like grown ass adults, not this bickering bullshit you're aimin' for."

After throwing some clothes in a bag, I gather my deodorant and shaving kit before making my way back to the woman waiting on my couch like Doomsday has arrived. How are we going to get our shit sorted if she feels defensive every time we talk? I need to stop being such a hardass and hear her out. Then, after I sort my shit with her, I need to sort Rex's shit for him.

Man up, fucker, you have a son.

HITS KEEP ON COMING

I knew this day would come. I didn't know it would come like this. The truth will set you free. Again, one of those things people say all the damn time. The truth will not set me free here. Nope, the truth here will tie me to Rex permanently.

Shooter settles on the other end of the couch and stretches his left arm over the back as he relaxes into his space. "Talk."

"I don't think I have to say it. One look at my son and you know the truth."

"Oh, no, baby, you need to say it. Not just for me to hear it, but I think you haven't faced it for yourself. I'm tryin' real hard here, Tessie, to keep an open mind. Take me back and tell me the whole story."

"Shooter, have you ever believed in something so much you couldn't see it any other way until it was too late?"

"Yeah, I made that mistake once. It cost me everything."

His honesty shocks me. I expected a simple yes, not that he has lost in his past.

"Rex was everything I thought I wanted. Only, well… only he wasn't. I'm white trailer trash from a broken home. Rex is the bad boy. Yeah, I watched him around here and there while I was going to high school. He was sexy in that wild, reckless way. I came from nothing and had no real future. As soon as I was legal, I sought out Rex. He had flirted with me here and there, nothing serious, but I was young and stupid. I didn't realize Rex flirted with anyone who had a pussy. I thought he wanted me, so I threw myself at him at first, but he denied me."

"Rex denied you?" Shooter can't believe me. Hell, if I hadn't been the one on the receiving end of the rejection, I wouldn't believe it either.

"Well, that made me want him even more. Before I left for college, I practically begged him to take my V-card. Looking back, I was pathetic. It wasn't great, but I had heard girls talk and no one had a good first time."

Shooter looks at me wide-eyed yet says nothing.

"Well, I wanted to make it memorable. So when I would come home from college, I would hook up with Rex. The first time may not have been good, but I wanted to make sure when I looked back on the man I gave my virginity to that I could at least say it got better. I kept coming back for more waiting for it to get better. Well, the sex did get better, but the situation between Rex and I never changed."

I feel my face flush in embarrassment as I realize I am talking about my sex life with the sexiest man I have ever encountered. Sure, Rex is hot. Rex is sin walking, talking, and fucking. However, Shooter is stealth. Shooter is the man in the shadows. He is the mystery that keeps you needing more.

He nods at me to continue.

"I was trying to be smart, you know. I went to the campus clinic. I was on the depo shot for birth control. Well, I had midterms and missed getting my shot. Then I came home for spring break, not thinking about it. Just like always in those two years since I first fucked him, Rex and I hooked up while I was home."

"Have you ever been with anyone but Rex?"

Shooter questions then shifts in his seat. "Never mind, don't answer that. It's not my business. Continue."

"I finished that semester and came home for summer vacation, but my period didn't come, which didn't shock me after being on the shot for so long. Then, I started getting sick to my stomach. My mom swears she saw a difference in my face. Either way, she point blank asked me one-day mid-summer if I was pregnant. She had seen me coming and going with Rex. When she asked, it made my brain go, *wait a second...*" I pause to gage Shooter's reaction, but he is unreadable. Does he think I am stupid?

He raises an eyebrow for me to continue.

"Well, I was knocked up. I tried to talk to Rex. Thing is, Rex and I never did much talking, and he wasn't ready to start then, either. He thought I was going back to college, so I let him believe I returned when I didn't. I stayed home, only going out for doctor's appointments. I didn't show until the very end of my pregnancy, and even then, I wasn't big. Keeping it quiet wasn't as hard as I thought it would be. Rex never came looking for me. I realized I always came home and sought him out. After I had Axel, no one really asked me any questions, so I didn't have to answer anything."

"Rex knows now. He's talked about your son. How did he find out?"

"Kids aren't cheap. I needed a job. Having no real education to fall on, I went to Ruthless and got a job from Bob. When Rex came in the bar and saw me, I tried to resist him at first. I told him I have a baby at home now. Then he told me all the things I wanted to hear. A quick fuck in the stockroom..."

The stockroom. My breath hitches, pulse racing, the panic rising. I can't breathe. My chest hurts. The room spins.

"Inhale, baby," Shooter's voice breaks through my thoughts. Sliding over the couch, he wraps his arms gently around me, pulling me to him. "Exhale. Tessie, you're safe. Inhale. I got you. Exhale. You're with me." His voice soothes something inside me as I follow his command. "Inhale. Stay in the moment here with me, baby. Exhale."

I blow out a breath as my body and my mind settle. I will get past this. I am stronger than what has happened to me. The stockroom isn't the problem. Shep, he is the problem. He can't get to me. Shooter has me. I feel his arms tighten around me as I calm down once again.

"You okay?" he asks in genuine concern.

"Yeah, I'm getting there. Anyhow," I add needing to continue, "Rex said the right things, and we fell into a weird routine of hooking up whenever he was home and didn't have some barfly on his dick. He's never asked about Axel other than common casualties." I tuck my hair behind my ears while I work to calm my nerves.

Pulling out of Shooter's embrace, I sit back against the arm of the couch while he consumes the middle and into part of my cushion.

"Why haven't you told him?"

"Rex doesn't want to be a dad."

"You didn't give him a chance. How do you know he doesn't want to be a dad? Is it the club, the lifestyle?"

"Yes, no… It's more Rex, not the club. I don't want to hold Rex back. He's not ready to be a dad. For a long time, I told myself I was waiting for him to settle down. I just knew he would pick me, and we would have this happy family. He just needed time and freedom to be wild. In time, I grew tired of it, tired of waiting. Sure, I know I'm the only one he comes back to, but Rex doesn't make sure I'm okay. Sure, he makes sure I get off, but beyond that, he doesn't check on me. If he cares so little for me, would he really do more for my boy? For a son he never asked for?

"Rex is not a selfless man. He's not going to give up his life for me and Axel. It wouldn't be fair of me to ask him, either. Time passed, and it was easier to let go of Rex and not worry about telling him. One day, I know I will have to, but I was waiting on Rex to grow up, and for it not to be me forcing him."

"Fuck, Tessie. You've kept the man's son from him.

Whether Rex was ready or not, it wasn't for you to decide. He's the boy's father and has a right to know." Shooter does nothing to hold back his irritation with me.

"I know it's a lot to ask, but please don't tell him, not just yet. I promise to tell him, but let me find my way to do it."

Shooter's phone ringing interrupts us.

"Shooter," he answers. There is a pause before he hands the phone to me.

"Hello," I say into the receiver, caught off guard as to who is on the other end.

"Tessie, I need you to come home, now. I can't feel my left leg."

"On my way, Momma. Don't move."

My heart breaks as the hits keep on coming. I knew I needed to be stronger. I never should have told her what happened to me, even if she got a watered down version. My problems can't be her problems.

I silently pray as tears roll down my face.

Fate, Karma, God, whoever is listening, please have mercy on my momma. She's a good woman. This disease is ravaging her body. Don't take her mobility away completely. Let her get through again without major complications. My stress did this, I triggered her flare up. Punish me, but please not my momma. She's all I've ever had; don't put her through more.

"Momma needs me. I gotta get home, Shooter."

SHOOTER

Seeing Tessie absolutely desperate to be at her mom's side tugs at a place deep in my soul. I never thought I would feel like this again. I want to take all her hurts away.

While I don't agree with her decision to keep Axel from Rex, if I tell Rex, I add to her pain right now. If I don't tell him, on the other hand, I'm betraying my brother.

Right when Tessie gets home to her mom, I'm called to sermon by Tripp. Leaving Tessie my car, I climb on my bike and head to the meeting. She has her car back, but I feel better if she drives mine. I can't leave to pick her up if she gets stuck right now. Should she need to take her mom to the hospital, she needs my car.

Everything is piling up, not just Tessie's needs. I have other responsibilities. I need to go in to work soon.

Ryder has two cars waiting for me. I have taken extra days off to be around for Tessie; as a result, I am backed up at work. Ryder is understanding, but that doesn't mean I still don't have a job to do.

Filing into the sermon, we are short a few guys who are on a run for the club. More importantly, they are on a ride to intercept a transport the Ghosts arranged.

"Update time. Keep your eyes open, boys. We've lost the Ghosts four affiliations. They are rerouting some of their dealings, which means we need to be proactive in setting up our alliances. We have disposed of their product in two shipments they will be picking up in the next few days. If they are coming to the South, we are gonna squeeze them until they hand over Shep. Shooter, we need you to call your guys in the Regulators to keep an eye on those South Florida transports. We can't have enough allies and extra eyes right now."

"Affirmative. I'll grab a burner and contact Ice."

When you survive together, literally putting your life in the hands of your military brother, you build a bond that will survive both time and distance. While Bowie left the Army to go back to the Savage Outlaws MC, my buddies Ice and Hammer started their own motorcycle club in South Beach. The Regulators are a badass bunch of no nonsense, ex-military bikers that now run Southern Florida.

Ice is exactly what his name says he is—cold. He is

a lethal man with a mind for business and skirting the law. Hammer, his VP, has an iron fist and a name for himself in the underground world. Hands down, I would trust any one of those guys to give me correct information and watch my club's back.

Tripp fills us in with the regular club business before dismissing us. Then, grabbing a burner, I make the necessary call to my ex-teammates and head home to Tessie.

Walking in, I round the corner to the kitchen and stop in my tracks. Tessie is at the table with Axel. She has those little chocolate morsels lined up in front of her and her son, a pan of raw cookies on the other side.

"Okay, Axel, if you have four chocolate chips and you add two more, how many chocolate chips total will we be putting on the top of the cookie?" Tessie asks her son.

"One, two, three, four... I eat one" —which he proceeds to do before continuing— "five, six. We have six chocolate chips on top of that one, Momma."

I smile at the sight before me.

"You didn't share with me," Tessie jokes.

"Momma, you ate like half the bag mixing the cookie dough. You gotta save some for Gigi," Axel defends.

"Axel, a woman can never have too much chocolate," Tessie informs her son.

"Always remember that, Axel," I add, making my way farther into the room. "It applies to all women, and it may get your ass—I mean, butt, outta trouble one day."

When Tessie laughs, my heart skips a beat. It is the most beautiful sound my ears have ever heard. I've never, in all the years at the bar, heard her laugh. Watching her with her son, the light in her eyes, I want nothing more than to protect what the two of them share.

"You're like the smartest dude ever, mister," Axel greets me, laughing alongside his mom.

"Nah, just observant. Learn early, chocolate is man's best friend, not a damn dog."

"Momma says damn is a yucky word. I'm not allowed to say it. She says it a lot when she stubs her toe and stuff."

If I am going to be around Axel, I need to work on my language. I have a feeling he will stay on top of me about it, though.

My mind goes back to Rex. Would he be willing to change to be a better influence for this little boy? I am unable to answer that.

Tessie starts to clear the table and puts the cookies in the oven. Watching her bend over, I can't help wanting to stand behind her. The luscious curve of her ass is one that other women should envy. Her hips are those of a woman who has carried a child and are made for a man to grip as he bends her over the bed, the table, and anywhere else he can have her.

Fuck, I can't think like this. Calming my chub from becoming a tent in my jeans, I try to think of kittens, turtles, hell, snakes, spiders.

"Momma says you're gonna be around for a while. What's your name, mister?"

His voice is the distraction I need from my lustful thoughts of Tessie. "Name's Andy, but my friends call me Shooter."

"Shooter, huh? Do you know how to shoot a gun?"

"Yeah," I answer simply.

"Awesome," Axel replies with excitement. "Maybe we can be friends after all."

Maybe we can, Axel, maybe we can. If I could get your mom to be in such easy agreement, it would make my life simpler.

WAR

Tessie

Mom's disease leaves me feeling helpless. I watch while she fights to be the woman she once was. I sit back, unable to help her as she faces the reality of her limitations. She has good days and bad. We hold tightly to the good outweighing the bad. She wants so desperately to be the pillar of strength she was for me growing up.

I wish I could find a way to show her she is stronger now to me than ever before. To know that she doesn't give up, she doesn't just rollover and let MS win, that makes her tougher than nails. I can't say I wouldn't succumb to the comforts of my bed and never get out if I were her. Hell, it takes everything I have to go out and get Axel to and from school some days.

Work, oh work, a battlefield in my mind. I can't bring myself to go back to Ruthless. Living off my money from Brinkley's is fine as long as we stay with mom.

She worked hard to pay off the house. Her car is as outdated as mine, but she doesn't drive much these days because the numbness in her legs gets so bad. Therefore, thanks to my mom's forethought and financial planning, I am able to survive on a part-time waitress's income. I have had to excuse myself a few times from work and had to leave twice because the anxiety was too much.

Right now, I am sitting in Shooter's car outside the diner, waiting for my shift to start. I should go inside, but being around people doesn't appeal to me right now. I am not a social butterfly on a regular basis; however, since the night of the attack, I find it even more difficult to associate with anyone outside of my house.

Push through it, Tessie, I coax myself. If Momma can wake up every day and still fight to do regular activities, I can get inside and serve lunch to these customers.

The rumble of a Harley startles me. Instinctively, I look around, my pulse racing. Shooter starts his bike daily and the noise doesn't faze me, but away from home, it sends my blood pressure skyrocketing. My breathing is unsteady and too fast as the panic attack seizes me. Even knowing there's no way Shep could be here, I'm unable to calm down, my body trembling. With sweaty palms, I pick up my phone and dial the first person I think of.

"Tessie," Shooter answers on the first ring.

I can't get the words out. I can't catch my breath. No words escape, no sound comes out except my heavy, rapid breathing.

"Exhale, baby," he coaxes. "Inhale, Tessie. Calm down, baby. Exhale," his voice soothes me.

I hear the phone shuffle. "Ryder, I gotta take off, man," Shooter says to someone in the background.

"Inhale again. Deep, slow breaths, baby. I'm on my way."

"No," I manage to squeak out.

"What happened, Tessie?"

"I… I… I," I stutter, unable to calm my breathing enough to talk.

Blowing out a breath, I try to settle enough to stop him from coming here.

"Inhale, baby. It's okay, Tessie. Just stay on the phone with me."

Dammit! I am so frustrated. Why do I allow myself to depend on him? How does he calm me so easily?

"I'm better. No need to come," I manage to get out, even if the strain in my voice gives away my struggle to settle down.

"Look around, Tessie. There should be a black sedan near you in the parking lot at Brinkley's. Boomer is watching out for you. You're safe, baby. Please calm down and tell me what has you so upset."

After a few minutes, the trembling stops, and I am back in control of my emotions. Looking around, I easily find and maintain eye contact with the black sedan. Only now I feel ridiculously stupid for getting so worked up and then reaching out to Shooter.

"I heard a bike, and I don't know… I thought about him. It just got to me. I'm sorry for bothering you with this. Oh, my God, I'm such a pain in your ass."

"Never be sorry for ever calling me. Baby, no apologies here. Shep, he's not gonna come around you. I promise he won't get to you again." Something about the way Shooter says it makes me believe him. I truly believe he won't let Shep anywhere near me.

"I'm late for work. I gotta go," I say, needing my escape.

"Don't ever hesitate to call me, baby."

"'Kay," I manage to whisper before sliding the phone off.

Blowing out my breath, I set about getting inside and to work. This cannot consume me further. I survived. I cannot allow it to hold me back from my life.

SHOOTER

"Got it bad this time, brother."

"Fuck off, Boomer," I reply, not trying to hide my agitation.

"Took off from work when you knew she was okay, drove straight here, hugged her, and now watchin' her work."

"Shut it, Boomer,"

"She's a hot thing. After what she went through, you're her hero, man."

"I'm no one's hero."

"I beg to differ," Boomer states in all seriousness.

Boomer was part of my team. He knows me better than most and takes that liberty to be brutally honest with me. He got out of the Army two years ago, and after spending a year riding the open highway, he came to visit me and stayed. His brown hair is in need of a cut along with the shave he is overdue for. Boomer likes his shaggy look, but don't think the man isn't put together in his mind. He is setting down roots here in Catawba and prospecting for the Hellions.

When my phone pings with a text, two words pop up: *Sermon Immediately*. Something is going down.

Tossing some money on the table for Tessie, I make my way to her.

"Gotta run, baby. See ya tonight. You need me, you call. If I can't answer, Boomer will."

She nods her head and I take off. Unfortunately, I can't answer my phone in sermon. I will leave my phone with Boomer, should Tessie need someone. Since she started her shift, she seems to be busy; therefore, unable to dwell on what is going on around her. I doubt she will call, but I would rather be safe than sorry.

A thought hits me. Could the bike she heard have been Shep? Did they find him? Is that what a sermon has been called for?

Wasting no more time, I break more than one or two traffic laws as I make my way to meet with my club. Within forty-five minutes of the message, we are all assembled.

Tripp calls the meeting to order, his face not hiding the contained rage he is battling within.

"Gonna keep this short and simple. Got a message," Tripp barks out at us.

After a swipe and a few clicks on his phone, a video plays. Slice, one of our drivers, is tied to a chair, his arms restrained with zip ties to the arms of the chair.

"Your club is now our enemy. Not by our hand, but by your own. We all face choices. Tripp, your brother has been delivered unto us. We captured him during your raid of our recent shipment. You may have gotten our goods, but we got your brother. The sins of one should not fall upon the shoulders of the innocent. Shep will not be handed over, no matter what my brother Thorn's orders are to the crew." Preacher's sick laugh fills our now silent room as we watch the video, helpless to do anything for Slice.

"Joshua 21:44. *And the Lord gave them rest on every side, according to all that he had sworn to their fathers, and no one of all their enemies stood before them; the Lord gave all their enemies into their hand.* The Lord delivered you unto our hand, Hellion. We have been given rest. And now the Lord hath delivered our enemies to our hand," Preacher recites the scripture in his sick, twisted version.

Then he pulls a knife out of his waistband. Taunting Slice, he cuts across his forearms. Four cuts on each arm for the eight shipments we have taken from their club. Slice fights against the unrelenting restraints as his arms bleed out, grunting in pain.

"By these hands, you stole from my family. By these

hands, you pay," Preacher rambles on while he produces a machete off a nearby table.

Tripp's chest rises and falls heavily as his breathing increases, watching our brother helpless to do anything. When Preacher raises the machete and slams it down, blood splatters the video screen as we hear Slice scream out in pain.

"As the Lord delivered our enemy to our hands, we deliver your own hands back to our enemy. His hands will be all you get back."

The screen goes black as the room fills with aggression and anger.

"Everything they say about Preacher is true. The fucker is crazy or on something. And his ramblings are gibberish. None of that bullshit he spouted makes sense," Kix pipes up.

"He punished the club for our antics in pushing Shep out of hiding. We have attacked their entire club for the 'sins of one,' meaning for what Shep did to Tessie. We are their enemy. In that fucker's head, God delivered us to their hands, so Slice was given to them for what we have done. It's twisted and goes against anything the Hellions would do. Thorn has ordered Shep to turn himself in to us, but the order is being ignored or no one knows where he is. Either way, Thorn is fucked from both outside his club and inside," Head Case explains.

Tripp is still staring at the now blank screen,

breathing heavily. "I want Shep out of hiding. He will pay for Tessie and now Slice!" He looks to me. "You call every contact you have, both on the right side and the wrong side of the law. I want Shep brought to us. We are puttin' that fucker in the ground by our own hands. Thorn needs the message that I'll kill every fucker it takes to get to Shep. I'm done playing with his transports and his money. If they want blood, it'll be their own I spill."

"If the Outlaws and the Regulators can't find him, Lock can. Lock, though, he won't flip for us. He's gotta stay clean in this," I inform Tripp of who I can reach out to easily. Lock is a cop and stays in touch pretty regularly.

"I don't give a fuck what we have to do, who we have to owe, you get Shep here. Call every marker we have. Make it happen," Tripp orders.

"On it."

My mind runs wild. Slice was a good man, and without having medical treatment, he most likely bled out in that chair while they did who knows what else to him. There is no way they let him live.

I step to the back of the room while the others continue to discuss how fucked up in the head Preacher is. Picking up a burner phone out of the file cabinet on the back wall, I dial the man with the most contacts. I reach out to the Regulators.

"Alibi," Ice answers.

"It's Shooter. I need a secure line."

"Negative," Ice replies. "Clean it up or tread water. Heard you got yourself an ol' lady," he laughs.

At his comment to 'clean it up or tread water,' I know he is telling me the line is secure, but he is not in a position to give me free replies. Therefore, I proceed with only tidbits of information so he can get started yet not give anything away to any ears listening around him. The mention of my ol' lady lets me know he is aware of my situation to some degree. Doesn't surprise me; the Regulators MC have more contacts on both sides of the law than any club.

"I need to find someone who is underground."

"Toilet problems happen to us all, brother. Little wifey doesn't like dealin' with shit, either," Ice states, letting me know he understands I need to flush someone out of hiding to take care of Tessie.

"Shep from the Desert Ghosts MC, Dana Shepard is his legal name."

"Get a fuckin' plunger, and I'll call a plumber. You got a mess on your hands."

Well, I do have a mess on my hands, but at least he will make a call for me. Ice will get the intel on Shep's location or scare him enough to walk right up to our clubhouse of his own free will to avoid the connections the Regulators have.

Turning back to my club, I give Tripp a chin lift to let him know it is under control on my end. Waiting is the hardest thing. Some of the guys want to go in, guns blazing, after the Ghosts. However, Tripp is level-headed enough to know we have to plan our attack, especially if Thorn really has no control over his club right now.

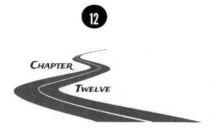

CHAPTER TWELVE

SECRETS REVEALED

S omething is going on. Shooter came home after my shift last week and moved us all into his house. This whole 'club business' shit gets real old, real quick. Not that I need to know every detail, but when my safety is an issue to the point that I have to uproot my son and my mother to protect them, then damn, some information would be helpful. Granted, I haven't come right out and asked questions either. Would Shooter give me answers or shut me out?

I can't complain, or at least, I shouldn't; Shooter is keeping us safe. His house is amazing with the three bedrooms, two full bathrooms, and the family room with a fireplace a girl could fall in love with. His kitchen is a dream to cook in, and he has a full dining room with a table that could seat eight. Everything about his place screams family home, yet he lives here comfortably alone.

The rooms and door jams are wide, easily accommodating Momma's wheelchair when she needs it. Shooter, ever the gentleman, has moved to his empty room on an air mattress so Momma could have his room with the bathroom connected. He was sleeping on the couch the first couple of nights, although I tried to get him to let us all share one room. I would've given Momma the bed and slept on the floor with Axel, but since he wouldn't let us do that, I went and bought the air mattress and set it up for him two nights ago.

Axel is on a cot in the second bedroom, something Shooter had stored in his garage. With Shooter being ex-Army, Axel is obsessed now with becoming a soldier like him. He thinks sleeping on a cot in our room here is the coolest. The room is void of decorations. The cot doesn't get in the way since the space only houses a bed, small dresser, and single nightstand. Everything is minimal.

Honestly, out of the nine nights we have stayed here, Shooter has ended up in his guest bed with me. Too bad needing to be strong for my son doesn't keep the nightmares at bay. I end up crying out in the middle of the night or waking up in a panic. No matter how quiet I try to stay, it's like Shooter can sense it. He ends up holding me until I fall back asleep.

There is something about him that soothes me. He carries himself in a collected, calm, and controlled manner at all times; maybe my subconscious is drawn to that. As long as I am wrapped in the safety and comfort of his strong arms, I sleep without waking and without the nightmares.

Deciding to be as helpful as possible, I have given his already spotless house a spring cleaning. Light fixtures are cleaned, floors scrubbed, and vents dusted. With there being so little furniture cleaning is relatively easy. Feeling like I need to do more, I venture into doing laundry for Shooter. Mistake.

Don't ask a question you aren't prepared for the answer to. Don't go in a man's drawers, whether to innocently put laundry away or not, unless you are prepared to pull out some skeletons from his past.

The black velvet box in his sock drawer is haunting me. I have pulled it out and put it back more times than

I can count on both my hands. The soft fabric under my fingers is a firm reminder this was once a gift for someone very special. The temptation to open the tiny box, to test the hinge, to touch the silk lining I am sure is inside, is almost too much to resist. The box is an enticing temptress. I keep going back to it.

Someone at some point in time meant so much to Shooter that he bought the contents of this box for her. In all the years I have watched Shooter leave the bar, he is mostly alone. The more I think on it, he has never arrived with anyone on his arm. Sure, I have seen him leave with Corinne a couple of times and a few of the other barflies, but Shooter isn't like the others. He isn't in your face with his sexual conquests. Someone had him at some point, though: hook, line, and sinker. He was there, ready to give them everything. Why does that pull at me so hard?

I am fumbling with the object of my curiosity when there is a noise behind me. Shit! I scramble, dropping the box at his feet.

"Baby, do I even want to know?" Shooter questions gently.

"Ummm… it's not what it looks like." God, I am so stupid. Of course it is exactly what it looks like. I was messing in his personal belongings, only I found it innocently, not because I was intentionally snooping.

"Can't say I know what it looks like. How 'bout we

don't beat around the bush and you just tell me why you had a ring box in your hands in my bedroom?"

Always honest, always blunt; he never plays games with me. Will he hate me for questioning him? This is beyond any of my business.

"I found it," I reply truthfully.

"Where exactly did you find it?" he questions, picking up the object of my fascination. Opening the box, I see the sparkle of a small, emerald cut diamond engagement ring. "Never mind. I know where you found it."

"I wasn't snooping. I washed your clothes and went to put them away when I came across the box," I try explaining.

"Tessie, just drop it." He closes the box and wraps his hand around it tightly, his eyes appearing haunted. Watching him, my heart breaks.

"Where is she?" I boldly ask.

"Dead," he replies, void of emotion.

"Shooter—"

"Drop it, Tessie. It was a long time ago. I'm sorry you found this. Thank you for doing my laundry." He walks past me, returning the box to his drawer without another word. To further solidify his point that our conversation is over, he walks into his bathroom, closing the door without so much as a glance backwards.

In this moment, it dawns on me how little I know about this man, a man who has held me at my very worst. What have I done to support him back? Not a damn thing. It's time for this to change. It is time for me to give to Shooter as much as he gives to me, at least emotionally.

SHOOTER

How do I explain Tracie to Tessie? She would love me saying, '*I know you can't sleep until I climb into bed and hold you, but my ex shot herself because of me.*' I am sure Tessie would sleep really well then... not.

I never thought about her doing my laundry and finding the engagement ring. Hell, I forgot I had the thing. Yet again, Tracie has come back to remind me of what I won't have.

Unable to avoid her in my house all night, I take a shower and make my way into the kitchen. Tessie, Claire, and Axel are all at the table working on Axel's homework.

"What's up tonight, Axel?" I ask in my new routine of finding out the daily activities of a first grader.

"Homework is stupid," he replies candidly, making me laugh.

"What's wrong? Homework is important, not stupid," I lie, knowing damn well I always thought homework was stupid, too.

"I gotta do this worksheet, but Mom says I can't use my answer."

When I raise an eyebrow at Tessie in question, she shrugs her shoulders at me and drops her head.

"What's the worksheet about?"

"*My Dad, My Hero* is what it's called. The teacher says we can draw a picture of our dad or our hero. Then, tomorrow, we have to stand in front of the class and tell all about our dad or our hero."

With two words, my gut twists uncomfortably. How does Tessie deal with this? He has to ask questions. What do the other kids think of Axel? It is not his fault his dad isn't ready to be a dad and hasn't been given the opportunity. I need to talk to Tessie about Rex. He needs to know. I will support her through the transition and explanations.

"What's your answer, so maybe I can understand what the problem is?" I question, not really sure how to help the situation.

"You're my hero, Shooter."

His words are a kick in the gut. I am far from being

a hero. I look at Tessie as tears fill her eyes, making it obvious they have already had this conversation.

Axel continues cheerfully, "You make my momma laugh and rest when she's tired. Momma never gets to be happy. You give that to her, Shooter. That makes you my hero. You take care of my momma. I don't have a dad that's around. I've never met him. I can't pick my dad so I have to pick my hero. Momma says my hero can't be about her though. She says I can't draw you, but I already did.

"Momma takes care of everything, and I mean everything. She cleans my room, she makes me food, and she makes sure I get a bath so I'm not the smelly kid at school. No one takes care of Momma till you. Tell her you're my hero, Shooter. Tell Momma I can leave it like it is."

Looking at Tessie, I see the tears roll down her face. Claire is wiping her eyes as I look at the bright blue gaze of the little boy at my table, pleading with me to make it okay for me to be his hero.

Walking over, I put my hand on Axel's shoulder and nod at Tessie so she realizes I am going to give in. How can you say no when his reasoning is out of love for his mother? She is raising a smart, little man. A strong, little boy who knows what he sees, what he feels, and doesn't hold back. A little boy I could only dream of having for a son one day. To be his hero is an honor greater than anything I have ever had.

"You can leave it, buddy."

Really not wanting to do anything to upset her, he looks to Tessie for reassurance, and she nods her head in agreement. She has raised him all on her own to be this amazing, little boy. Does she see what a wonderful job she has done? Probably not. No one has been there to support her and show her just how great she is doing. What would things be like if Rex were in the picture?

The decision made about his homework, we clear the table of schoolwork to sit down for dinner together. Thinking this day couldn't have any more emotional challenges, we all get a little too comfortable. Tessie is cleaning the kitchen after dessert while Axel takes a bath when the rumble of a Harley coming up my driveway draws my attention outside. Thinking it is most likely Boomer, I don't react to it. Going to the front door, I open it to find Rex pulling up.

Fuck! I step out on my wraparound porch and shut the front door. Leaning against the railing, I wait for my brother to dismount. I meet him at the bottom step, hoping to ward off any thoughts he has of inviting himself inside.

"Shooter, I came by to check on Tessie."

"She's fine. Thanks for stopping by," I try dismissing him.

"I've tried callin' her. She won't answer me. I wanna talk to her."

"Tonight's not a good night. Tomorrow don't look good, either."

The audacity of him to show up here now is appalling. He's had his chance to step up and be a man. He should have been the one to claim her, but he didn't. Now he comes to my fuckin' house to mess with her head? Hell no!

I don't get a chance to dismiss him again. The front door flies open behind me right before a pajama clad Axel runs out.

"Shooter, time for my bedtime story!" he excitedly announces our new routine.

I watch as the recognition dawns on Rex's face.

"Fuck!" he roars, his tone stopping Axel in his tracks.

CHAPTER THIRTEEN

BROTHER NO MORE

R ex's yell draws my attention to the front door. Stepping to the porch, I watch as the man who has captivated my mind, body, and soul for years recognizes the little boy on the bottom step. There is no denying who fathered Axel, never has been. He came out looking like the spitting image of Rex.

"Axel, come inside," I instruct, because my son's face is full of fear at the rage rolling off Rex.

Thankfully, my boy listens and takes off into the house to find my mom. I stand on the porch numbly as I watch Rex ball up his fist and swing, connecting with Shooter's jaw. I watch Shooter stumble at the impact before another swing then contact to the other side of his face. He grabs his head and forces it down as he brings his knee up. Crack. I hear the sound of Shooter's nose breaking as I see the blood pour down his face.

I cry out for him to stop while Shooter takes every single hit as they just keep coming. The tears run freely down my cheeks. One after the other, Rex is beating the hell out of him, and Shooter doesn't make one move to fight back. With blow after blow to Shooter's sides, he stumbles to stay upright and continues taking every hit Rex is gives.

Unable to watch further, I step down off the porch. Adrenaline courses through me as I reach the men. Without a second thought, I pull at Rex's arm as he aims to swing yet again.

"Stop it," I beg. "It's my secret, not his."

Rex turns to me, his eyes filled with pure hatred, his knuckles bloody. I flinch as I see his hand go back. Before he can hit me, Shooter has reached up and grabbed his arm, yanking it behind his back so force-fully I am certain his shoulder is dislocated as he grunts in pain. His other arm wraps around Rex's neck, holding constant pressure while allowing him to breathe.

"No, fucker. You can beat the shit out of me all night long, but you will not raise your hand to her. She's the Goddamn mother of your child, and you will not fuckin' touch her, ever. Be pissed. I get it, but you don't get to hurt her any more than you already have for the last however many years," Shooter says as Rex slows his fight against the hold Shooter has him in.

"Fuck off, Shooter. You've been playin' house with my family."

"Your family? I've never been nothin' but a whore to you." I can't believe he would say that after he almost hit me. I don't know the man being held captive in front of me.

"Go inside, baby," Shooter instructs calmly. "It's all gonna be okay. Stop crying, please. Go check on Axel; make sure he didn't see any of this."

How can he be so calm? He just got the ever loving shit beat out of him, letting Rex get his aggression out on Shooter's body so he wouldn't take it out on me. Why does he do so much for me?

SHOOTER

My lungs burn with every breath I take. I am pretty sure I have two at least bruised if not broken ribs, and my nose is most definitely broken. Blood fills my mouth as I am sure I lost a back tooth. Once I hear my front door shut, I release the hold I have on Rex.

"I'll stand out here all night and let you take it out on me, but you almost put your hands on the mother of your child tonight, Rex. Tame that shit." I spit out the blood on the ground beside me.

"Fuck you, Shooter! Don't you dare fuckin' tell me what to do."

Wrapping my arms around my ribs, I wince in pain. Rex is pacing around my yard now, muttering obscenities.

"I know it don't make a difference, but I planned to

tell you. With the war with the Ghosts, though, I wasn't sure it was the right time. Tessie, she's been through so much these last few months."

"Shut the fuck up, Shooter. You're my brother. Dicks before chicks, bastard."

"Listen to yourself. You're as much a child as the little boy she's raisin'. Tessie was tryin' to let you have your life. She thought being a parent, when you weren't ready, would hold you back. She didn't want to inconvenience you or disrupt your lifestyle, so she's been waiting for you to be ready. She's been waitin' on you to grow the fuck up."

"That's my blood running through that boy's veins and no one told me."

"I know this is a shock. It took me by surprise, too. But you scared your boy tonight, and his mom and I need to clean up. Axel isn't goin' anywhere. When you have taken the time to take all this in, we'll work this out."

"Don't you blow me off, motherfucker! You should've told me."

"It wasn't my secret to share," I state honestly.

"Fuck you, Shooter. She kept my son from me. You kept my son from me. Brothers no more." His final words are another punch to my battered soul before he spits at the ground by my feet then goes to his bike and takes off.

REX

My world stopped spinning the moment I laid eyes on the dirty-blonde haired, mini me. How did I not know? How could she not tell me?

Throttle down, I speed down the open road of the night, running from my life. In the blink of an eye, everything has changed for me.

The secrets. The years of hiding him. My mind races. I can't say Tessie has point blank lied to me about her son…

Her son. Fuck!

Our son.

My son.

I have a son. I am a father. Drexel Devon Crews, a dad. Shit, what's his name? Did she think to give him my name? Is he a Crews?

Pops, my grandfather, the man who stepped in as my

dad when I didn't have one—it is his last name both Tripp and I carry. Does my boy carry on our name?

Pops would be ashamed. *Treasure your woman when you find her, boys,* he always told us. I didn't listen. Nope, I have followed my dick around to every hole open to me in North and South Carolina. Yet, I have always found my way back to Tessie. She has been the one person to take me exactly as I am. No matter how many times I disappoint her, fuck around on her, she has always had my back and been there. She has always been my safe place to fall. What have I done? Ruined her, ruined the possibility of us.

Worse than that, she needed me and I turned my back on her to fuck with Shooter's head. I knew he would claim her in that sermon. Why would I step up and give up the freedom of my life, my world, when my brother would step in and be the good guy?

Why would she tell me about my son? I have never given her the opportunity to tell me any of her problems. Sure, she has lain in bed with me and listened to me bitch about work or life. She has taken me anyway she could, and I tossed it all away.

What have I done to show anyone that I should be a dad? Sure, I am hard working and loyal to my club, but what does Tessie know about that? How can she know about my dedication to all things Hellions when I can't even talk about ninety percent of it with her?

The white lines of the road pass under me as the miles tick by. I am going nowhere fast, both on the road and in my mind.

"Be men to be proud of. Actions speak louder than words, boys. When you do wrong, and believe me, you will do more wrong than right some days, you own up to it. Completely. You can't take back the stone once it's thrown. The reality is, you can never really right the wrong once it's done. It will live on forever in one's memory. You can atone for it. You can work hard to assure you never make the same mistake twice. But there is a time for freedoms and a time for life responsibilities. Be the man to handle his responsibilities. Be the man to take responsibility for his shortcomings and failures. Take pride in being humble enough to admit when you are wrong and when you have failed." Pops' words from a childhood fishing trip play in my head.

I have done wrong by my boy. I have done wrong by his mother. If Shooter hadn't been paying attention—if he hadn't stopped me—I would have hit the mother of my child, the woman that has raised him completely on her own, all to allow me to have my life without the burden of responsibility.

"People will think many things of you. Some true, some complete lies. Their opinions don't matter. The half-truths, the lies, the many things people will think of you throughout this life should never hold weight. It is

what you see in the mirror looking back at you that should tell you the character and the man in which you are. Look in the mirror, boys, and be men to be proud of."

If I looked in a mirror right now, there would be no pride. There would be shame. I let my son down. Tessie had no right to keep him from me, but in my actions I showed her I wasn't responsible. She believed I couldn't or wouldn't be there for her. I caused that. I have to own my mistakes here.

I have to be a better man to raise my boy into a man that can look in the mirror with pride and humility. I have to raise my boy to be the man Pops raised me to be.

RETRIBUTION

Turning my back to the man that just took a beating because of my secret kills me. Realistically, I need to check on my son. He has never really had a man around. Sure, we visit my grandfather, but it's not often enough for him to be an influence on Axel. Other than teachers at school, my son has not had a male in his life until Shooter.

Shooter, my unexpected hero. My friend. My confidant. The first man to really support me with no agenda. The first man to accept me just as I am, broken and all. He knows my every secret and doesn't judge me.

He wanted to tell Rex; however, out of respect for me and the life I have built for myself, he kept my secret. Rex came here for who knows what and Shooter could have thrown me under the bus. No, instead Shooter let Rex take out his rage on his body.

"Momma, who is the man outside?" Axel questions me.

I am unprepared to answer. I have parented with the belief that I didn't need to overwhelm him with explanations. If he was curious enough to ask a question, I would answer it simply and honestly. Only, the answer to this question isn't as simple as saying 'that's your dad.' I don't know if Rex will want to be a dad even though he knows about Axel now.

"He is someone Mommy knows from work. He is Shooter's friend." I extend my arms to my boy for a hug. "Time for bed."

"I want to wait on Shooter to read to me like last night. He does the voices and shit—I mean, and stuff."

"Axel," I chastise his language slip up.

Shooter tries to catch himself, but he doesn't always. Kids are like sponges, and Axel adores Shooter, so I know this is part of that.

"Sorry, Momma. He makes it really cool, though. Can I please wait for him?"

Not knowing how long Shooter will be or how long it will take for him to get cleaned up, I decide I need to get Axel to bed before he comes inside. The last thing my son needs to see tonight is the sight of Shooter banged up. Thank goodness my mom is here.

"How about you snuggle buggle with Gigi tonight? I think she misses her special time with you."

"I really wanna have Shooter," Axel pleads.

My son has really bonded with this man. Has he needed this all along? Why isn't there an instruction manual for this? I feel like I have messed up so much. Was I wrong in keeping my son from having this? Yes, I was, but I can't confidently say that Rex would give him what Shooter clearly is now.

If I had just put my big girl panties on and faced Rex all those years ago, Shooter wouldn't be a bloody mess right now.

"Not tonight. Gigi hasn't felt well, and I think she needs a pick-me-up that only you can give her."

"Gigi does love cuddles. Will you tell Shooter good-night for me?"

"Sure thing, love," I reply, smiling sweetly at my son.

"Tell him it's the good cereal for breakfast tomorrow. None of that oatmeal you keep trying to feed us, Momma. We are men; we need more than oatmeal."

I laugh as he takes off to spend time with my mom. Just in the nick of time, too, since Shooter walks in, holding his shirt over his nose to clean up the blood. With his shirt off, I can see his ribs are bruising already, and from what I can see of his face, it's a swollen mess.

Following him into the kitchen, I watch him pull down a first aid kit. Silently, I stare in amazement as he pushes his nose back into place as best he can. I am sure there will be a bump left behind.

Walking over, I take the kit out of his hand. He doesn't speak to me as I begin to run water in the sink.

"I'm gonna get a wash cloth. I'll be right back to clean you up," I whisper.

Dropping the shirt from his hand, he reaches out for me, grabbing my arm gently, and my body comes alive.

He is shaking his head at me. "Go to bed, baby. It's been a long night. We can talk tomorrow. I'll clean up." He lets me go and turns to wash the dried blood from his hands.

"I'm sorry I brought my mess to your doorstep. Shooter, let me take care of you like you have me."

"Tessie, don't be sorry; especially not for this. You did what you felt you had to for your son. Rex will figure his shit out in time," Shooter comforts.

When he tries to walk past me to go get the wash

cloth, I place my hand on his tense abs, stopping him. I lick my lips as I take in the close proximity between us. He is breathing heavily from his injuries, and on every inhale, he flexes his muscles under my soft fingers. Even bloody, this man is sexy as sin. Could I go there? I can't believe I can even think of it after my attack six months ago.

The moment passes as he begins to move past me once again. Placing both hands on his stomach, I only put enough pressure to keep him in place, but he still winces slightly.

"Let me, Shooter. Please." I need to do something to help him. Every time I fall apart, he has been there to pick me up. The least I can do is clean him up. When he came to get me for Rex, the night my car broke down, I seriously doubt he was signing on for all of this drama.

Finally, he steps back to lean against the counter, nodding that I can go get the cloth. Returning, I begin to clean his face before putting a butterfly strip across the crack on his nose. I hope it holds the cut together while it heals. Blood had fallen on his chest, so I wipe it away as I take in the one tattoo Shooter has on his now battered rib cage.

It is a bible verse. 1 John 4:4. *"Ye are of God, little children, and have overcome them: because greater is he that is in you, than he that is in the world."*

Without thinking, I reach out and touch the script, causing him to tense under me and hiss at the contact.

"Oh, sorry. I'm sorry, just sorry." I begin to cry for all the pain I have brought this man, both physically and emotionally. I know the ring pulled at something deep inside him. I just want to make this better for him.

I reach over and grab gel pack to put in the freezer to get cool for him. Until then, he will have to make do with frozen peas.

"You should probably go to the hospital."

"Nothing they can do. My nose is reset. It has to heal, can't do anything more. My ribs are bruised, possibly cracked. Again, nothing they can do," Shooter states as if this happens all the damn time.

Wanting to check him over thoroughly, I take Shooter's large, calloused hand in mine. I know he didn't hit Rex back, but he grabbed him to keep him from hitting me, something Rex has never done before. Lesson learned. When a man is full of rage, stay out of the way.

"What's going on in your head, baby? I can see the wheels turning through your eyes. You're concentrating mighty hard on my hand." Shooter brings me back to his mess of a face.

"Your tattoo?" I question trying to keep our conversation in neutral territory.

"The bible verse was my first tattoo. Being in the Army, doing what I did, I didn't have tattoos so I wouldn't have recognizable markings. No discernible features. Then I got out, I went through some shit and needed a reminder not to be caught up in this world, material things, status, and such. When I patched to the Hellions, I got the insignia inked on my back. Other than that, I'm a blank canvas. Now that we've covered that, tell me what you're really thinking?"

Damn, nothing gets by him.

"Why are you doing all this for me?" I ask with genuine curiosity.

"I told you. I wanna be friends, simple as that."

"I'm not worth the trouble," I whisper, meeting his eyes.

We stare at each other silently for the longest time. Watching him, I feel like he is trying to reach into my soul and consume me as he continues to drink me in. Then his hand comes up, tucking my hair behind my ear before coming to rest behind my neck. Gently, he squeezes the back of my neck before he brings his swollen forehead to rest against mine.

"Baby, you're worth everything," he whispers before pulling back and kissing the top of my forehead then releasing me.

SHOOTER

"Talk quick, Bowie. I need headphones," I answer my phone, letting him know I have listeners nearby.

Tessie is with me in the kitchen. Since it is Saturday, Axel is home, watching a movie in my room with Gigi. It has been four days since the altercation with Rex, who hasn't said a word or reached out to either of us. Does he really not want to be a father to his son?

Tessie and I discussed it and if Rex reaches out, we will work it out for him to be a part of Axel's life. I have to say I am disappointed in him right now. I know it was a shock, but ultimately, I thought he would want more from this. Tripp hasn't shown up or called me, so I don't think Rex has shared the news with anyone yet.

"Got a package for ya," Bowie states.

"How?"

"Word got around we were visiting you. Ice made some connections and sent word your package has been stuck in the same zip code. Decidin' to be friendly-like, I picked it up for ya. Three clicks and a right. It'll be waitin'."

"Good deal. I'm on it."

Tessie is watching me. Does she know that call was about her attacker? Am I that transparent? He is here, just three miles down the road in an abandoned cabin on the right, way back in the woods.

Bowie is in town with his woman and Tin Man, his brother. They needed a place to hide out, so I put them in Tessie's old trailer. In case Tessie wants her independence back when this is all over, I contacted the landlord a while back. She agreed to hold the place for Tessie, but I have been paying the rent and utilities to make sure it stays available should she want it.

Ice knew Bowie was in town, and since Shep would be on the lookout for Hellions, it was smart of him to get Bowie's help. Shep never would have seen the Outlaws coming.

My heart races as adrenaline flows through my veins. Retribution will come for Tessie. Vengeance will be mine.

I tug Tessie to me, pulling her against my chest, and flinch as my ribs scream out in pain. Wrapping my arms around her, I hold her to me. She doesn't miss a beat, bringing her arms around my back and hugging me. She is so small against me. I breathe in her scent before kissing the top of her head, then I pull away.

"Gotta go out, baby. I don't know when I'll get back."

"Okay," she whispers.

As I am walking out the door, she looks at me with tears in her eyes. "Be safe, Shooter. Come home to me."

Immediately, I turn back to her. Placing my hands on her neck, I tip her head up to me, and without giving it a second thought, I bring my lips down on hers. When her hands come up to grip my wrists and she relaxes under me, I swipe my tongue across the seam of her lips. As she opens her mouth to me, I deepen the kiss as my tongue searches out hers. While my thumb rubs the pulse point in her neck, I feel her heart race in beat with mine. I pull back, sucking on her bottom lip before releasing her mouth.

"It's gonna be okay, baby. No worries," I state before I release her and make my way back out.

In the garage, I grab my burner phone and contact Tripp with the location to meet me. Then I pull my nine mm, checking it quickly before getting on my bike and pulling out of the driveway.

Does she know where I am going? I hope to hell not. She will never forget that night and what that sick fucker did to her, but I want her to find a way to move past it, to live again, to find happiness and laugh. I want Tessie to laugh every damn day for the rest of her life, not be haunted by the memories.

Arriving at the cabin, I am met by Bowie and Tin Man out front. I manage nothing more than a nod in greeting before the sound of Harleys in the distance have me on alert. My body cries out in protest at all the movements I am making since I am still healing.

When the bikes get within range, I relax, knowing it is Tripp, Rex, and Kix.

"What the fuck happened to you?" Tin Man asks me while we watch my brothers file in.

"It was deserved, leave it at that." How else am I supposed to answer the questions of why I am still black, blue, and in some places, varying shades of yellow and purple? I kept a secret from Rex. If the shoe was on the other foot, I would kick his ass, too. I got what I deserved and took it, enough said.

After my brothers' park and make their way over to us, Rex walks straight past me to the front door without a word.

"What the fuck happened to you, brother?" Tripp asks me.

"Another time, another place," I reply, not wanting to face the wrath of my club prez for the betrayal of my brother right now.

He nods at me in understanding.

"Problems, Bowie?" Tripp questions.

Looking at Bowie, I see his shirt is torn and there is blood on his hands and side.

"Nothin' I couldn't handle. Crazy fucker got a nick in, no big deal. He's knocked the hell out and chained. Gotta get back to Shay, but you know how to reach me if you need me." Bowie hands me keys before making his way over to his own bike.

Tin Man gives me a chin lift and follows his brother as they prepare to leave.

By the time I make my way over, Tripp, Rex, and Kix are already at the door to the tiny cabin.

"You two are tied to Tessie. Kix and I'll stay on guard out here. Give the fucker what he's got comin' to him." Tripp orders leaving Rex and I to face Tessie's attacker with the freedom to do with him what we wish.

We enter to find an empty, open room with no windows. There is a mattress in the corner on the floor, but other than that, the space is completely empty. Shep lays on the floor, unconscious with his hands cuffed and chained to his ankles. He is as dirty as ever; his clothes covered in filth, his stench filling the room and letting us know that he hasn't showered in days.

He starts to move, and Rex is automatically standing over him. As Shep opens his eyes slowly, Rex kicks at his legs, making just enough contact to show he's there.

"Wake up, fucker. It's deliverance day."

Shep groans. Then, before I can move, Rex is at him, pulling him up by the chains. The energy in the room is reckless; rage radiating off the two of us.

Rex stands Shep up against the wall where his knees buckle, and he drops back to the ground. Doesn't look like his gunshot wounds healed well. This is probably why he remained in the same zip code hiding out. Rex yanks him back up and pins him in place with his forearm against his throat.

"You know why we got you, Ghost?"

I get closer to watch as Tessie's attacker answers for his crimes.

"Pussy. You got me for pussy." Shep smiles back sickly, his face changing to one of a man lost in a memory. "Sweet, tight pussy," he adds, describing Tessie.

Unable to control myself, I am at his side. "That sweet, tight pussy is *mine*. You touched my ol' lady, you motherfucker," I state, meaning every word out of my mouth. That pussy he touched is mine. Tessie is mine.

The monster inside me wants out. The demon in me needs to watch this fucker die. My lungs burn as my breathing becomes heavy. My sides ache because my injuries aren't healed enough to exert myself like I want to.

Taking a step back, I move just in time. Rex releases

Shep only enough to put his hands on Shep's shoulders and knee him in the crotch.

"How's your dick feel now? Don't worry; I'm nowhere near done playin' with you."

Shep coughs. "You had that tight cunt. You know it's good." He makes eye contact with Rex before glaring at me. The man has balls.

Rex brings Shep's head down to slam his knee in his face. His face gushes blood as Rex tosses him backwards onto the hard floor beneath us. Landing on his back, he stares wild-eyed at the two of us standing over him. He shakes his dirty hair, trying to get the mangled mess out of his bloody, rapidly swelling face. The sick bastard then brings his cuffed hands up to his mouth, sticking two fingers in his mouth before he sucks. Smiling at Rex and me, he moans in pleasure.

"I can still taste her blood and juices mixed together. Tight ass, too. She's a delicacy. Shoulda killed me that night, Shooter, not left me with two bullets in my legs. I've gotten off *every. Single. Night* since to thoughts of your ol' lady."

In response, Rex raises his boot covered foot up and stomps straight down on Shep's crotch. Twisting his heel, he grinds down. While Shep curls upward in pain, vomiting on himself and Rex's boot, Rex pulls a switchblade, ignoring the mess.

He grabs Shep's hand. "These are the fingers you

touched the mother of MY SON with! Goodbye, fucker."
Rex slices his fingers off and tosses them over his
shoulder.

Blind rage has consumed my brother as something
inside me goes wild at the mention of Tessie's son.

Moving to my knees, I grip Shep's head in my lap.
He twists, trying to pull away. Forcing his head between
my knees, I hold him in place while using my thumbs to
force his eyelids open.

"Look at me, fucker. Something given or exacted in
punishment—retribution. This is yours. Vengeance is
mine. You touched the wrong one," I state, releasing his
eyelids.

Picking his head up, I twist to the right until his neck
breaks. Dropping his head with a thud to the ground, I
roll back on my feet and hop up.

It is done.

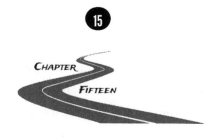

CHAPTER FIFTEEN

MONSTER IN ME

SHOOTER

T*ainted. Ruined.* I am a black soul. Killing Shep won't cause me to lose sleep tonight. He deserved what he got. Would Tessie see it that way, though? Would she have peace knowing her attacker won't harm anyone else?

Stepping out of the cabin, I need fresh air. There is a part of me that is still unsatisfied. I want nothing more than to turn his body into an unrecognizable pile of skin and bones. However, mutilation of a dead man's body is not my style or the Hellions. We aren't assassins, we aren't cold-blooded killers. When the club has to murder, it is in defense or as a punishment fitting the crime committed.

Bikers live by their own code, not by the laws of our judicial system. That is why I patched with the Hellions in the first place. They aren't swayed in courts, a screwed up political system focused on one's financial gain. The Hellions are a brotherhood, a family taking care of their own. Not one of our members is on any form of government assistance. We all have regular jobs, or we work for one of the club owned businesses. Every patched member pays dues annually to the club. When something goes to a vote, every vote counts equally, an officer does not carry more weight than a patched member. Officers carry more responsibility and get a larger cut of the club profits, yet they have no more pull in a vote than I do. Sure, they make decisions without a vote for the best interest of the club, but they have earned that when they were chosen for their positions.

Being a Hellion isn't about a patch. I am a member of a brotherhood, a family. One that has each other's backs, a family that stepped in and wouldn't back down in seeking justice for an innocent woman.

Tessie should have never been in danger. Working at a bar doesn't mean she is a whore. Sure, she was dressed somewhat provocatively, but the way a woman is dressed is in no way any indication she is available. It gives no man any right to assault her.

Today, Tessie and every other girl Shep has touched in his past were given justice. I would do it again in a heartbeat, too.

While Rex comes outside to stand beside me, Tripp and Kix are handling getting the message to Thorn. Lighting up a cigarette, I inhale the nicotine, trying to bring my adrenaline levels back down to normal. Rex stands beside me, blowing out his own smoke.

"Feels good to finally do something half way right by her," Rex opens up to me.

"She's a good woman, Rex," I reply, unsure as to how to answer him or where he is going with this conversation.

I don't know what to say to him about any of this. If he is waking up to what he had under him this whole time, where will that leave me? Where do I want to be left? Will my first kiss with her today be my very last? If Rex wants her, will he get her?

"Take care of her, Shooter."

"What the fuck are you talkin' about?" I question, my annoyance growing. He seriously won't turn his back on them after laying eyes on his son, will he?

"She cares about you in a way she never did me. She's comfortable with you in a way I never allowed her to be with me. I fucked it all up. Do you live with regrets, Shooter? Have you ever looked at your life and realized your choices ruined someone else?"

I only nod in agreement, not knowing where he is going with this.

"She was working at the bar because of me, but she had dreams, real damn dreams once. When I first laid eyes on her, she had this innocence to her. Not because she was a virgin, but this real innocence about life. She came from fuckin' nothin', but she worked hard and was gonna be a nurse. I don't know if she told you that or not. She was goin' to college, but her momma couldn't afford that shit. So, Tessie got scholarships, got loans, and made it happen. She was innocent to life's cold, harsh realities. She had dreams, though, and she was chasin' that shit. I knew it. I shoulda left her alone, but no, selfish that fuck I am, I didn't." He takes a drag off his cigarette.

I look over at him as he stares off into the now night sky, continuing to smoke.

"Man, she always put me first, but she was nothin' more than a convenient piece to me. She knew it and held onto hope for a long time. Then she said no more, but I didn't believe her. I failed her on more than one occasion, and she lost everything because of me."

"Rex, I don't think she sees it that way. Axel is everything to her. He's a damn good kid, too. A little too much like you sometimes, but still, she's done right by him." My body relaxes as I think of Tessie's son, a boy that has awakened a part of me I never knew I had.

"I wanna get to know him."

"He wants to get to know his dad."

"Dad, fuck that sounds strange."

He doesn't have to say that twice. Tracie's voice sounds in my head. *"Dad, can you imagine, Andy? We could get married and have a baby. You could be a dad. Wouldn't you like that? The Army can't be forever, our baby would be, though."*

I shut her down that night. I even had the fuckin' ring in the center console of my truck. I didn't propose, though. Nope, I didn't marry her or give her a baby. Instead, I crushed her.

"Tracie, I have a career. I can't marry you until I know you can handle my life as a soldier. Damn, don't cry. With what I do, having a family runs a risk. You could be used for leverage if I was ever captured. I need to know you are strong enough for this before we get married and add a kid to the mix."

"See, Andy, you can't give life. You are a black hole. A bottomless, heartless pit of hell inside. There is a monster inside you that doesn't give life. No, Andy, you don't believe in giving a life, saving a life. Just taking, that's all you do. No, the boy I once knew is gone. The man in front of me just takes. You take my love, you take my sacrifice, and you take for granted that I can't go on

without you. In the name of your service, your duty, your country, you take lives. In the name of love, you won't give that up for me, for our love, for our future. I have dreams, Andy. You killed my dreams."

"You got this, brother. Tessie has raised him right, and she'll want you to be around him. She just needs to explain it to him. But this is another hit for her, so let me talk to her and allow her time to prepare. I'm not saying it was right by you, but she hasn't had it easy by any means, either," I tell Rex, needing to stop my thoughts from continuing about Tracie.

"Make things easy for her for once, get home to them. We'll handle the shit here; you go home and hold her close, take a burden off her mind. If she watched you leave, I know she's worried about you right now."

"It's not like that with us, man," I say, watching Rex be serious with me more than he ever has before.

"Then fuckin' make it like that with y'all. Do you know she's never asked me for one damn thing until she stepped in for you? She didn't call me to pick her up when her car broke down. No, she called Doll. She's never asked me for one fuckin' thing until she was worried I was gonna beat you to death. I saw it in her eyes: you mean something to her that even I never did. She deserves good, brother. Give her good."

Tessie

Women's intuition is a real bitch sometimes. My gut twists. I feel it in my bones. Shooter had this distant look in his eyes when he took the call. Emotions overwhelmed me. I can't help feeling it was about Shep. He will never tell me, though; I know that. I feel it with every part of me and can't deny it no matter what lie he may have to tell me.

There is this darkness inside me, a monster within that wants them to find Shep and kill him. A painful death, too. Not a quick gunshot to the head; no, that would be too easy. I want him to feel fear. I hope they make the bastard hurt. Does that make me a horrible person? Possibly, but the fuck if I care. Mercy has never been a friend to me, so why should she shine her good graces down on Shep? The bastard should get what he deserves.

By the time Shooter comes home, I am hanging by a thread. I have needed him to be okay. I have needed him to come home and hold me. I have never needed the comforts of a man the way I do from him. He looks tired, like he has battled a war inside his mind.

"Baby, we need to talk."

Those are four words no woman ever wants to hear. *We need to talk* never ends well.

Steeling myself, I prepare for him to send me away. Hell, if Shep is handled, there really is no reason for me to stay. I am so stupid. He left, took care of whatever, and now he can go back to his life without me, his life that wasn't full of challenges and chaos at every turn.

"Talk," I say. Might as well get it over with so I can go pack.

"I saw Rex tonight. He wants to see Axel."

Tears pool in my eyes as I stop breathing for a moment. He wants to be a part of this. Was I wrong this entire time? Did I cost my son years without his dad? Is Shooter going to send me away because Rex wants something more with me? I am done with him and the back and forth game we played.

Rex can have time with his son, but he can't have me. I want more from my man than he will ever be able to give me. In a relationship, I want the complete acceptance I have given Rex for all these years. I want the comfort, security, and unconditional caring that I have with Shooter. He has shown me in these months what it is to have someone who has your back without expectation. Rex can see his son, but beyond friendship there will be nothing more shared between us.

We have this weird dynamic. Without actually being together, Shooter has shown me what it is like to be in a healthy relationship - one based on caring, trust, and acceptance. These feelings I have for him have developed over time, and I don't want to lose what Shooter and I share. I want it to grow. Every touch we share is with care and consideration.

I can't let go of his kiss from earlier. Never have I kissed a man with such feeling inside me. Sure, I have been consumed by lust more times than I care to count with Rex, but kissing Shooter... I was consumed by passion and dare I say, love?

"Well, then," I start to say.

Shooter takes me by the hand and leads me to the living room before I can finish my thought. Slowly, he sits down on the couch while I move to sit on the other end, only his arms wrap around my waist and he pulls me to his lap. Half lying on the couch, he pulls my back to his chest and lays me against him.

"He is in a good place with this," Shooter begins, rubbing my arms gently up and down. "Relax, baby."

"Have you ever made a decision and knew that there would never be a right answer? That's how I feel about this. Rex deserved to know, but he wasn't ready. Maybe if I had told him sooner, things would be different."

"Do you want things to be different with Rex?" Shooter asks genuinely. There is no jealous tone, just honest concern for me.

"No. Shooter, I don't. Sure, I shared my body with Rex, but he was never there for me like I want my partner in life to be. Yes, he would ask how I was, but real feelings... No, we didn't share that. I thought for a time I wanted a relationship with him, yet that was an illusion based on my ideals of Rex, not the reality of the man. When I ended things, he didn't fight to get me back. No, he tried the same lines, the same moves from before. When I held strong, refusing him, he wasn't fazed. I don't want him to hate me, but no, I don't want things to be different with Rex."

"I want you, Tessie. You gotta know, though, there is a monster inside me. I'm plagued with the shadow of death. I've done things, and honestly, I wouldn't take a lot of them back. There was a reason for each circumstance but one. You gotta know, that one was a senseless loss, a selfish and unnecessary loss; one that was on my hands." There is a distance in his voice, a sadness that is haunting.

"Shooter, tell me. Tell me about the one that haunts your dreams. You know mine, share this with me. You carry so many of my burdens, let me handle half the load you carry."

"Baby—" he starts, but I cut him off.

"I know you can't tell me club stuff. I know you're an ex-Army sniper. But what causes you to twist and turn at night? It's in your past and keeping you from your future."

"I don't talk about things that can't be changed. This can't ever be changed. Baby, I'm not a good man."

Turning in his lap, I lay on my side, careful to not put a bunch of pressure on his still sensitive ribs. Reaching up, I run my hand through his hair as something nags inside me to get this out of him. Whatever is in his past is the only obstacle standing between us and our future together.

"Perception is sometimes skewed when you are too close to a situation. Tell me, Shooter. Share your darkest hour with me. Let me face your demons with you," I plead, feeling the need to be strong for him and help him through this.

"Her name was Tracie," he begins, and my heart breaks for him as he tells me about the love he once shared.

CHAPTER SIXTEEN

CONSUME ME NO MORE

"Shooter, you were young. You couldn't have known she was in such a dark place in her mind."

"Age doesn't matter. She loved me. I took her every dream away without giving it a second thought."

"Haven't we all been selfish at that age? Everyone is. I was. It didn't matter that Mom was sick and working two jobs to help me at college. I was chasing dreams. Tunnel vision gets us all at some point. You were focused on having a career. Very few eighteen-year-old boys know what they want to do and go after it; but you did, and she wasn't ready to handle that. Some people can't take change, and you were in a situation of constant change. Shooter, you can't blame yourself for her shortcomings."

His eyes watch me carefully. It is evident he has never talked about this with anyone. He has never allowed himself to see beyond Tracie's words.

Deciding to be brave, I move up and brush my lips against his gently. Breathing in, I take his bottom lip between my own and suck. His hands come up my sides as he kisses me back. Passion ignites, and I want so much more from this man. Pulling away, I watch as his eyes dance with lust and an emotion I can't read.

"Let go of her hold on you. Depression can easily consume someone. It's the darkness you can't escape, the silence that is so deafening. I heard you whisper to me in the night once. You know, about it. She was trapped in what she wanted and couldn't have, not seeing the blessings she held in her hands. You're an amazing man, Andy Jenkins, but you can't save the world. You can't pull someone out if they don't grab onto the hand being extended."

"Baby—" I cut him off with another kiss.

"You saved me when I was in the darkness. You held me how many nights, to remind me I wasn't alone?

You are my light. You are my strength when I have none left inside. When my mind was consumed by thoughts of that night, you helped me find my way out. Shep consumes me no more because of you. Let go of the hold she has on you."

His eyes dance with a need I can't read. Cupping his face in both of my hands, I kiss him again, deciding to hold nothing back. Our tongues tangle as I run my hands up into his hair.

Moving over him, I lay my chest to his and feel him hardening under me as his hands roam the curves of my ass. I could kiss him for a lifetime and still feel like it is not enough.

His hand comes up under my top, running along my spine. When he brings his hands up my sides, his thumbs run under the curves of my small breasts. I pause momentarily at the contact. He tenses under me, causing me to pull away.

"Baby, you okay?" he asks. His eyes are glazed over in lust, yet he is concerned for me.

"Yes. My mind went back to *it*...to *him* for a split second, that's all. You can't take it away. It happened, but I'm ready to move past it... with you."

Leaning up, I remove my cami pajama top, exposing my buds to him. I have never been large, except when I was pregnant with Axel. I have always been a B cup.

Shooter's large hands easily cover my breasts,

causing me to shudder at the contact. It has been so long since I have allowed myself to relax and feel pleasure in my body again.

I drop my head down and kiss Shooter again as he squeezes my breasts, causing me to moan as my panties dampen with desire. I need this. I need him.

Rocking my hips against his erection, I seek friction. He feels so good, so large, so all consuming.

Pulling away, I tug his shirt up and over his head, wanting to feel him skin on skin. His lips get tight as I forget about his ribs. Shifting, I can tell he is uncomfortable. He has one leg off the couch and uses it to slide himself farther upright into the corner of the arm of the couch. When he does, it moves me to straddle him.

As his jean clad erection hits my sweet spot, I rock my hips as I crash my lips to his, no longer caring to be gentle. Moving, I kiss his neck, nipping at his earlobe.

His hands roam my exposed skin, snaking down to my shorts. When he cups my ass, I grind into him, wanting more as lust takes over. He kneads my ass as I continue to dry hump him, unable to stop myself from wanting more. As his fingers brush along my pussy, I moan.

"Axel," he whispers. "What room is Axel in?"

Pulling back, I stop moving and look in Shooter's eyes. Is he trying to kill my libido? Does he not want me? His rigid cock makes it evident he wants to fuck, but maybe it's not me he wants.

Lifting up to sit on him, I cover my breasts with my arms, feeling my embarrassment creep up.

"My mom's room," I reply, not wanting to admit that I sent my son to sleep in her room because I wasn't going to be sleeping without Shooter being home. No way am I ready to admit my feelings for him. No way can I tell him that I depend on him. Can I?

Before my mind can wander further into the depths of my insecurity, I am placed on my feet from his lap. Shooter is quickly standing and taking me by the hand to lead me to the room I have been staying in. He shuts and locks the door behind us before going over to the bed we have been sharing. He unbuttons his jeans and unzips them to give his erection more room before lying down, pulling me down beside him.

"We don't have to do this, baby. Anytime you want to stop, we will. I'm not going to have you moaning or calling out my name where your son could walk out and find us, though."

Fuck! Will I ever learn to think? I let my hormones run wild and didn't give a second thought to who could come out to the living room and find us.

Sensing my change in thought, Shooter's lips crash into mine, sending shivers through my body. Needing more, I reach my hand down his pants and into his boxers.

He is thick and long when I wrap my hand around him and slide down his length. He kisses me harder as his hands slide my pajama bottoms and panties down. His pre-cum moistens the head, and I use it to lubricate my hand and continue to slowly stroke him, imagining how good he will feel stretching me.

As his fingers reach my exposed pussy, he teases my trimmed, narrow line of pubic hair, causing me to buck, wanting more contact from him. He cups my pussy with the palm of his hand and uses his fingers to tease circles on the muscles on the sides of my juncture, causing my wetness to trickle out.

I can take no more of his teasing as I rock into his hand. I whimper in need as I continue to slowly stroke him.

He pulls out of my grip and breaks our kiss. Then he drags his nose along my jaw as he breathes on my neck, making me tremble. My body is on fire for this man, all of my senses working in overdrive.

His fingers slip between my pussy lips, rubbing circles over my clit as I cry out for more. He licks my erect nipple and blows on it, sending more sensations through me. Then one finger slowly and delicately slides in me, and for a moment, my body tenses at the invasion. For a split second, my mind tries to go back there.

"Breathe, baby. Inhale," Shooter softly instructs, bringing me back to the here and now.

I run my hands through his hair before bringing his head back down on my breast. Taking my cue, he takes my nipple in his mouth as his tongue circles before he sucks. He begins to slide his finger out of me, but I clinch down with my inner muscles, silently begging him not to stop. He slides back in me and then out, coating my pussy in my own liquid as he continues to slowly tease me.

"Relax, Tessie. No rushing."

He trails kisses down my stomach then kisses his way down my legs. Making his way back up, he kisses the inside of my thighs before his mouth descends upon my pussy lips. He licks as he inserts two fingers inside me, stretching me, prepping me, and sending me over the edge as my body ignites under his mouth and touch.

He continues to lick and suck while he moves his hands to massage my ass while I ride the few after-shocks of my orgasm.

"Shooter, I want you."

His head comes up and he kisses his way back up to my neck before stopping to look at me.

"Baby, I don't have a condom in here, and I'm not sure your mom wants to see me like this."

"I have an IUD, and I'm clean. I've been checked," I spit out, not caring about how desperate this makes me sound.

"I'm clean, too. Are you sure?"

Reaching between us, I grab his cock, feeling his pulse run through it. I bite my bottom lip and nod.

Rolling to his back, Shooter lifts me over him. "With my ribs, you gotta do the work now, baby. You wanna stop, we stop. No questions, no hard feelings. You're in control, Tessie. Take what you want." He spreads his arms out, lying under me as my own personal toy to do with as I please.

Leaning down, I kiss him, tasting myself on his tongue and driving me wild.

Reaching between us, I rub his cock along my pussy, moaning at the contact. After I slide his dick in me, I sit up to allow my body to adjust to his size. I have never felt so full in my life. My heart wants to burst out of my chest as I join together with the man who has captured my soul.

Slowly, I begin to move up and down over him, steadying myself by holding onto his hips.

"You. Are. So. Beautiful," Shooter says as he watches me ride him.

Tucking my hair behind my ears, I feel nerves build up in me. Nothing has ever felt so good inside me before, but I am holding back because the emotions I have for this man are overwhelming me.

His hands come up to my hips and still me. "Never be nervous with me, baby. Inhale, Tessie. Breathe. Let go, baby. Let go and be with me." His words calm me, the way he knows me, knows what I need.

Dropping my mouth to his, I begin to move again, kissing him as I grind, causing my breasts to rub against his chest, sending more sensations through me. He rocks up to meet me, and we both pick up our pace as our need for each other becomes too much to deny. Unable to focus on kissing him, I pull back as my orgasm builds.

"Annnndddyyyy," I cry out, as my inner walls clamp down around him and my climax overtakes me.

I am still going through the aftershocks as he continues to pump into me, holding me steady while he finds his own release.

Dropping my head to his neck, I lie there with him still inside me as we both try to steady our breathing.

"Thank you, Shooter. That was... that was just... beautiful," I stammer out.

"You're what's beautiful, baby."

SHOOTER

The sunlight shining through the curtains wakes me. Finding myself tangled with Tessie is heaven. After a shower spent consumed in one another, we fell asleep with her in my arms. No nightmares plagued either of us. The sound of her even breathing keeps me from moving. I don't want to wake her, so I relax and treasure the moment.

The good things are made to push us through the bad. During all those deployments, the good would be what my team clung to in order to get through the mission at hand. Memories of Tracie would push me through. She had a smile that would light up a room. I would think of times she had really smiled, like our proms, high school football game parties, just going out four wheeling, or her watching me work at her dad's garage.

Her dad. I haven't spoken to him since the day of her funeral. Would he see things the way Tessie says they are? That I couldn't save her when she wouldn't even reach for the hand I was holding out?

The sounds of little feet coming down the hall draw me back into reality. The strongest woman I have ever known is lying in my arms, in my house, and her son is definitely looking for me to make certain he gets to eat some sugary cereal rather than the oatmeal his mom is sure to try to feed him. We have a deal.

Since he usually is on the cot and I always end up in here holding his mom, finding me in here won't be a surprise to him. Usually, I snake my way gently out from under Tessie and feed Axel the breakfast of his choice before she wakes up. However, today may be oatmeal day because there is no way I am giving up even one second of her being in my arms this morning. I need to know she doesn't regret last night.

Some mornings, she wakes before us, and some mornings, she ends up getting up alone. Today, she will not wake up alone. She's not a barfly or a random hookup. She won't wake up alone after we shared a night together. I know she had that in her past, and I refuse to give her that in her future.

Axel knocks on the bedroom door even though it is unlocked. He has never knocked before. Granted, that was at his house and he didn't know I was there. Tessie really has raised him with manners. As much as I would love to have her naked in my arms all day long, I am glad we both got dressed after our shower so Axel can freely come in.

I don't know how Tessie feels about us or what she wants for her son.

"Come in, buddy," I call out.

Tessie wakes up and, forgetting about my ribs, pushes off me, causing me to grunt in discomfort. After yesterday and then the activities of last night, I am a little more sore than usual.

"Sorry, Andy," she whispers.

Andy, huh? It has a nice ring to it coming out of her mouth. I smile as I think of her calling out my name just hours ago.

Axel comes and jumps on the bed between us.

"Shooter, can you make my breakfast?"

"No—" Tessie starts to answer at the same time I do.

"Sure, but how about we cook something for your momma and Gigi?"

Tessie looks at me with a smile on her face, knowing I am on the oatmeal prevention task force.

Axel is bouncing in excitement.

"Momma loves pancakes. Can we make those?"

Getting out of bed, I stand and stretch slowly, careful of pulling my midsection. My chest tightens at the sight of Tessie lying in bed with Axel sitting beside her, both of them smiling up at me. This is a happiness I have never felt before. More than happiness, this is true long lasting contentment. Happiness is an emotion that comes and goes, contentment is real inner peace. I could be completely satisfied waking up to these two every morning for the rest of my life.

"Let's go, buddy," I say to Axel as I lean over and kiss his mom on the forehead before we head to the kitchen.

"We gotta get fruit, Shooter," Axel states firmly when we start pulling out the pancake mix and pans.

"What's in the fridge?" I question, not having a clue.

Tessie wasn't in my house two hours before we had to go to the grocery store because apparently, beer, bread, and peanut butter were not balanced food groups to feed her family. Being a bachelor, those are common staples in my pantry.

"Momma says, if I'm gonna eat the sugary syrup, I gotta eat fruit. Otherwise, I'm gonna make my tummy grumpy. She says we gotta give it as much of the good as we feed it the bad."

"Well, she's right. You gotta keep everything in life balanced. The good shit—I mean; stuff takes care of the times we gotta go through the bad."

"You're the good stuff, Shooter. You balance us out, ya know."

"Nah, Axel, you and your mom and Gigi, y'all are

the best parts of my days. That's the good stuff, knowing I get to come home to that."

A thought hits me. How much longer will I get to come home to them? After Tripp talks to Thorn, the threat may be eliminated. What then? Will Tessie move out?

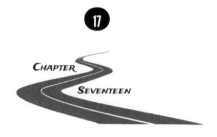

MENDING BRIDGES

F ailures happen for everyone, boys. Your measure
of success does not come in wealth; your
successes happen when you face your failures and learn
from them. Pops always told us not to give up.

"Where ya at, fucker?" Tripp kicks my chair at his
dining room table, jarring me.

"Right here. What the hell?"

"Doll asked you four times if you wanted a beer, and

you said nothing. Caroline agreed to have sex with you
—" My cousin is cut off at the screech of Lux.

"The hell I did, Tripp."

Grabbing my chest in mock emotion, I say, "Lux,
you crush me. We're all family here, you can be honest.
Doll is used to everyone wanting my cock," I joke,
knowing it drives Caroline crazy, especially when I call
her Lux.

"What gives, Rex? Normally, you would've grabbed
your junk and pushed the issue more," Doll, ever the
observant one, inquires.

Dropping my head into my hands, I blow out a frustrated breath. It's time to own my mistakes and face my
failures. I drag my hands down my face before I look up
and face everyone.

"I have a son."

The room falls silent and everyone stills. Well, not
exactly the reaction I was going for.

"What the fuck?" Tripp questions.

"Tessie's boy, Axel. He's my son."

"No way!" Doll exclaims, the shock written all over
her face.

"Don't mean this harsh, but you sure he's yours?"
Tripp asks with a look of understanding.

"I've seen him. One look at him, and there's no
denyin' it." I stand up, no longer able to remain still.

"Whoring around does that to ya, Rex. What are you

gonna do about it now?" Caroline has to put her two cents in as usual. That broad busts my balls every chance she gets.

Doll quietly walks over, wraps her arms around my waist, and softly asks, "Why didn't she tell us? Why didn't she tell you?"

"I need to talk to her. I sort of over-reacted to seeing him. From what Shooter has told me, she didn't think I was ready. She wanted me to live my life."

"Shooter? Of course he would know if it's that obvious. He's had the boy living with him. Why the hell didn't he tell you? I'll kick his motherfuckin' ass," Tripp says, throwing his beer into the wall, the glass shattering everywhere.

"I already tried," I say, giving them the truth. It is not fun to beat the shit out of someone who puts up no resistance.

"What the hell you talkin' 'bout? How long have you known? Shooter's busted face the other day, that from you?" Tripp questions, glaring at me.

Doll releases me to put her hands on Tripp's chest. "Stop it. This is for Rex to sort out and us to support him, not you getting in a rage. Damn."

"I've known long enough to do something about it and haven't done it yet."

"Are you angry with her? Tessie?" Caroline decides to join the conversation.

"I was, but I don't know what I feel or think now. I have so many questions." I turn to the sexiest woman I have ever encountered trying to remain calm as I still sort through this in my head.

"You want me to blow smoke up your ass and inflate your ego further, or do you want me to keep it real with you?" Caroline asks honestly.

"Lux, when have you ever done anything but destroy my ego? You wouldn't give it to me any other way but straight, even if I asked."

"If it were me, I wouldn't have told you, either."

"Caroline!" Doll does nothing to hold back her shock. "That's bullshit. As that little boy's father, Rex should have rights, and she took all his choices away from him."

"Get real, Drexel. Have you ever wanted a kid before one was standing in front of you?"

My actual name. Oh, she's seriously using the big guns to get my attention. I shake my head back and forth rather than actually answer her.

"If she came to you when she was pregnant, would you have supported her? I'm not talkin' money, either. Would you have made time for appointments and classes? When she was sick, puking her guts out from morning sickness, you were probably rolling out of some barfly's bed. You gonna stop chasin' pussy for her and her kid?"

I open my mouth to answer yet don't get a word out before Caroline is snapping at me again.

"Let me answer for you. No. Now, you would've given her money that much I know. You aren't a lowlife. She wouldn't have had to worry about bills. Hell, she wouldn't have been workin' in a bar if she would've told you. I know that much about you and Tripp. You take care of what's yours. Appointments, no, you wouldn't have been there when she had to pee on command. When she had to drink this sickeningly sweet, sugar drink for a glucose test, she would've been alone. When she went into labor, you probably would've been on a transport or balls deep in a barfly. Either way, you wouldn't have been there to watch her exhaust her body, bringing life to your baby boy.

"*If,* by some chance, you tried to be in a relationship with her, you would've kept her ass at home while you still did whatever the hell you wanted. She would resent you, and eventually, you would resent her for what you thought you might have missed. *So,* while all of you get angry at Tessie for not telling him, I say I would've done the same damn thing."

Closing in on her in her seat at the table, I pick up either side of her chair, pulling it out then turning it around while she sits in it, unmoving. Once I have her spun around, I put my hands back on either side of the chair seat cushion, caging her in. Getting eye to eye with her, our breaths mix when we exhale.

"You think you have me all figured out? Yeah, I fucked this up. How about this one for ya? You are right! I wouldn't have been there. Sure, I would've given her money, but no, I wouldn't have been at one single appointment. I can't stand here and tell you I would've made it a priority to be at the birth of my son because I didn't know about him. I can tell you that seeing what Tessie has gone through has shown me a lot of things. It's not just what she's gone through with my son, it's Shooter. She looks at him in a way she's never looked at me."

She claps her hands at me. "There, you were given a round of applause for seeing the error of your ways. Is that what you want?"

"You push me at every fuckin' turn, woman! That's not what I want."

"Then what do you want, Rex? Own it, right now, what do you want?"

"A woman to look at me like Tessie looks at Shooter, like Doll looks at Tripp. A woman who doesn't judge me and accepts me failures, flaws, and all. Since I ruined it with the one person who has ever given me that, I guess I need to find a way to earn it from everyone else. And that starts with earning acceptance from my son," I state firmly, not giving her a chance to back down from my stare.

"Then why are you still here?" she challenges.

"Good fuckin' question." With that, I take off without another word to anyone.

TESSIE

Tessie

Shooter is at work. Axel is at school. Mom is resting. Today, I have a quiet day. I am wiping down the kitchen counter when my phone rings.

"Hello," I greet, unsure what to say to the man on the other end of the line.

"Can I see you?" Rex asks.

"I'm at Shooter's house."

"See you in ten." The line disconnects before I can say another word.

Is this smart? Will he be in an uncontrollable rage again? He wouldn't hurt me, would he?

Needing reassurance, I dial the person I have come to rely on more than I have ever depended on anyone before.

"Baby, you okay?" Shooter answers immediately.

"Ummm…" I start to say as the panic builds. What

if Rex wants to take Axel from me? Yes, he was unexpected. No, I didn't have a clue what I was doing in the beginning. Hell, I still don't. But that little boy is my whole world. He can't take him from me.

"Breathe, baby. Talk to me, please," Shooter pleads into the phone, automatically soothing me.

"Rex is on his way over."

"You want me to come home?"

"Yes… No… I don't know. I just needed to hear your voice more than anything."

"Do I have anything to be worried about?" With my history with Rex and what we have being so new, I can't blame him for asking.

"Andy—" I start but am interrupted by his laugh.

"Nope, I got nothin' to worry about. But you can say my name again." Shooter chuckles into the phone.

"I'll say your name again tonight when you make me scream it."

"You're killin' me, baby."

His relaxed tone makes me feel centered, and I finally realize Rex has had time to sort stuff out in his mind. He won't come here to hurt me or yell at me.

"I'll be all right. Go back to work, just needed to hear your voice."

"You need me, never hesitate to call, baby. Don't talk with Rex too much, you need to rest your voice for tonight." He laughs again. I never tire of hearing him laugh.

Flirting with Shooter has me smiling until I hear the rumble of Rex's bike.

"Gotta go, he's here. I'll call if I need you. Thank you for always being my rock, Andy."

"You're killin' me," he whispers.

"Makin' sure you remember you're alive, baby," I toss back at him before ending the call.

For years, he has merely gone through the motions of his life. Tracie took a piece of him with her when she committed suicide. Slowly, I am going to get every piece of him back. Slowly, I am going to fill his days and nights with life and laughter. He has brought me back from the brink one breath at a time, and I am determined to give this back to him.

Walking to the front porch, I decide to meet Rex outside. Shooter's home—our home—is for us or I hope that maybe one day it will be. I won't taint it with negatives from either of our pasts.

Sitting on one of the rockers he has, I motion for Rex to follow suit.

"Tessie," he greets, looking nervous.

"Rex," I reply, unsure what I should say.

"About the fight. I never woulda hit you. Things may be different between us, but I wouldn't hurt you like that."

"Rex, I get it. Stepping into a man beating another man wasn't my smartest moment. Let's just get to it. We never have been one to talk much, so don't drag it out now. You look tired and like you got shit to say, so say it," I say, not toning down my bitchiness. I want to get this over with before Axel is out of school. I need to know what I am facing so I can start preparing for it.

"What's his name? His full name. I've been riding around all night and morning just wondering what his actual name is. I was at Tripp's last night, and I couldn't tell them my son's name," he asks while staring out into the driveway.

"Axel Devon Crews."

"You gave him my name?"

"When I found out fathers don't have to sign the birth certificates here in North Carolina, I decided to give him your last name. From the moment they told me I was having a boy, I knew he would have your middle name, but when given the opportunity to give him your last name, I took it. Rex, I know it's hard to believe, but I didn't mean to keep it from you for so long."

"Does he know about me?" Rex questions hunching his shoulders almost as if he's defeated.

"He knows his dad is a truck driver that does long distance transports. He knows you travel all the time. At his birthday and Christmas, I always give him a present or two from you, depending on my money. He always gets at least one thing signed 'Love, Dad'. I didn't mean to exclude you, but I didn't think you would want to be tied down. And I didn't want him to be left with disappointments if you weren't a constant in his life."

"Honestly, I don't know if you did the right or wrong thing because I don't know what I would've done if you would've told me. But I hate knowing you've struggled and given up so much. I want you to know I would've helped you financially, if nothing else." Rex still won't look at me.

"I don't need your money, Rex. I make due and always will. Axel doesn't go without the things he needs."

"I know. That's not what I mean. This isn't coming out right. Look, we gotta let go of the past. I did you wrong, and you have made the sacrifices for my mistakes. So, where do we go from here? Maybe I wasn't ready before or maybe I would've been. Either way, it's irrelevant. In the here and now, I wanna know my son. I wanna take care of him." He finally looks at me with sincerity in his eyes that hits me in my gut. He really does want to be a part of Axel's life.

"Okay. I need to tell him that you are in town. We can go to dinner together or something next week. How does that sound?"

"Sounds like a date," Rex replies with excitement in his voice.

"Rex, this doesn't change anything between us. We were over a long time ago. I don't want to go back to that or a twisted version of it."

He stands up and laughs. "I keep messing this up. I know it's over, Tessie. I'm still a work in progress, and you never looked at me the way you do Shooter. You are one strong-ass broad. He needs strong and you need a good man. He's a good man."

Coming over to me, he reaches down, taking me by the hands and pulling me out of my chair. Rex then cups my face, putting his lips to my forehead for what I know will be the last time. I close my eyes and breathe him in. When he pulls away, there is a sadness in his eyes I have never seen before.

"Thank you for my son. Thank you for standing by me and now, for changing my life." With those words, he turns and walks away, leaving me with tears pooling in my eyes.

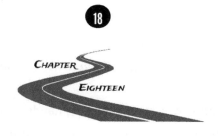

VISITING

"Do you think it's too much for Axel to meet Rex tonight with a friend? I know they aren't together, but will it confuse Axel more?" I ask Shooter, as my anxiety climbs.

"Breathe, baby. It's gonna be fine."

"I need an opinion, Annndddyyy," I drag out his name in sarcasm.

"Keep sayin' my name, baby, and we won't make it to dinner on time," he retorts with a wink.

Putting my hands on my hips, I give him my best *I'm being serious* look. Yeah, that lasts two point five seconds before I am smiling at him. What can I say? The man makes me happy even when I am stressed to the max.

He walks over to me, puts his hands on my hips over my hands, and pulls me to him. I have to tip my head back to look up at him.

"It will be fine. Caroline has some stuff going on that Rex is helping her with. More friends for Axel; look at it that way."

"Guess it's time to face this," I whisper before Shooter kisses me breathless.

Ending our kiss, Shooter says, "Come on, Momma, it's gonna be okay. We don't want to be late. Axel is excited."

I am not a fan of those kid's pizza places with all the tokens, games, and prizes. The germs all over the machines make me want to give Axel gloves. Normally, I don't have enough spare cash to take him to a place like this, but Shooter and Rex both agreed this would be the easiest way to transition Rex from stranger to friend, and eventually, the goal of being a father.

Deep breaths, Tessie, I coach myself as we walk into the establishment.

Axel is bouncing on his feet with excitement to be here and meet his dad. I, on the other hand, want to puke.

Rex will be good with him when he is around, that I don't doubt. Will he be around consistently, though? Axel deserves better than someone being in and out of his life.

"Inhale, baby. Exhale and let it go. I see the wheels turning in your head, but it's gonna be okay. I'll kick his ass before I let him bail on Axel after starting this. Trust me to take care of you both," Shooter whispers to me, giving me the security I need.

We make our way to the table where Rex and Caroline sit with a crappy pizza, drinks, and more tokens than one kid could possibly spend in a day sitting in front of them. Doing my best to push through, I smile in greeting at both of them.

Rex stands and hugs me. Having two patched Hellions in a place like this isn't common. I have to push back my insecurities because I feel people staring at us.

"Hey, Tessie, thank you for this."

"I didn't do it just for you, Rex. Axel needs his father," I state, as he backs up to greet Shooter in one of those handshake, man hug, back slap things they do.

Tears pool in my eyes as I watch Rex then squat

down to Axel's eye level. Matching eyes stare at each other in amazement.

"Hey, Axel, I'm Rex. You ever been here before? It's my first time."

"I came once for Jeffrey's birthday party."

"My friend Lux over here, she says kids like this kinda shit. I'm a big kid at times, so we should have some fun. You good with that?"

"Momma says shit is a bad word. You shouldn't say it," Axel interrupts, causing Shooter to laugh behind me.

"Tame that right now, Rex. He will get you every damn time," Shooter adds, winking at me.

After all of us laugh together, easing the tension, we spend the next two hours playing games, laughing, and earning tickets to turn in for silly prizes. Early on, Axel would only go play games with Shooter, but in time, he warmed up to Rex, and the two of them really seemed to connect.

Getting back to Shooter's house, I can't stop smiling as my son seems to be transitioning through all of this okay.

Axel is in the garage with Shooter, 'tinkering' as Shooter calls it. Axel calls it 'guy stuff that you wouldn't understand, Mom'. This has become another part of their routine. In the evenings, while Mom or I cook dinner, these two go hide out there, turning wrenches and whatnot.

Making my way out to check on them, I smile as I hear them talking.

"Hand me the tire gage, buddy. We gotta check the tire pressure on Gigi's car."

I hear the shuffling of my son moving around to get the proper tool.

"Shooter, who taught you about cars? Was it your dad?" my boy asks curiously.

"My dad wasn't the most mechanically-inclined. Great man, but he didn't care about what made something work, just that it worked. When I was a teen, my parents said I had to buy my first car, but I didn't have a lot of money. I had a girlfriend whose dad was a mechanic. I bought a piece of sh—crap truck, and it kept breaking down. Fred didn't like his daughter bein' out with me and stuck, so he took me under his wing and helped me rebuild the engine and then eventually, paint it. I ended up quitting my fast food job and working for him after school and weekends."

"Will you be around to rebuild a truck with me? You know, when I'm old enough."

My heart breaks at my son's innocent question. Will Shooter be around? I can't imagine not waking up with him. The reality is, we have been here far too long. Even Mom said it was time for us to go back home.

Before Shooter can answer, I make my presence

known. "Hey guys, time to get cleaned up. Axel, you've had a busy day and need a bath and to go to bed."

My mind is still going over how to talk to Shooter about us moving home while we go through our night-time routines. Getting Axel tucked into bed, I am surprised at his question.

"Shooter, can I meet Fred one day? Do you think we could go to his shop sometime?"

"You would want that?" Shooter wonders, a mirror to my own thoughts.

"Well, I know Rex is my dad and all, but you kinda are, too. I think it would be cool to see the shop where you learned all that stuff. If we can't, it's no big deal."

My heart shatters. Shooter and I need to have a serious conversation about what we are doing here. What does the future bring? It is not just about me and never has been. This time, it won't be me alone feeling the loss. What have I done?

SHOOTER

Talking with Axel and thinking back on Fred has me unable to sleep. Getting up, I make my way out to the garage where I run my hand over the old, blue toolbox in the corner, my mind going back.

"Boy, that's my baby girl you're takin' out. You keep breakin' down, and it's not to be missin' curfew, it's cuz you really break down. We can't be havin' that, son," Fred told me the first week I had my truck.

My dad was a factory worker, my mom a stay-at-home mom. We didn't have much, but we were comfortable. My parents taught me that, with hard work, you will persevere. Fred taught me patience. Fred taught me you don't give up when at first you don't succeed. When I decided to join the Army, my parents and Fred were encouraging me every step of the way.

I haven't seen Fred since the memorial service for

Tracie. I refused to speak to him that day. What could I say? His wife had passed on years before, then his only daughter took her own life because of me. He lost what he had left of his wife because of my decisions.

"You okay?" Tessie asks me from the garage doorway.

"Couldn't sleep. Sorry I woke you."

"Talk to me," Tessie says, walking over to me. "Is this about us?"

Trying to avoid the subject, I reach out and pull her to me. I allow myself the freedom to kiss her, letting us both be lost in each other. When I pull back, she runs her thumb across my lips.

"I've been the one to be lost in before. I've been the one that was there for him to forget his troubles, too. I'll be that for you, but I want more. Talk to me. Let me listen. Let me be your shoulder. Don't let my body be your escape alone. Don't let that be all we share. Let me walk through fire with you until we come out on the other side. Don't shut me out."

Her reminder of the way things were with Rex cuts me deep. I don't want her to feel that is what I am doing here. Deciding to open up I share with her more of my past.

"Fred is Tracie's dad. I don't know how he would feel about meeting Axel. Hell, I don't know that he ever wants to see me again."

"Won't know if you don't try, right?"

"You make it sound so simple." She smiles at me in reply.

I have never been as open with anyone as I am with her. "There are some things I've learned in the last year. If we don't take a chance, we will never know what the end result will be. If we let the mistakes and traumas of our past define us, we will never move forward into our future. I want my son to know that, when the hits keep on coming, you don't give up. You push through and come out stronger on the other side.

"Yes, Fred may not want to see you. Or he may *need* to see you. I would like to think you care about my son. I would like to think Axel means something more to you than just being my son. I would like to think that, if something were to happen to me, you would still be a part of his life. Fred lost his wife and his daughter all too soon. Why did he have to lose you, too?"

Rubbing circles on her pajama covered hips with my thumbs, I find comfort in touching her. I find hope in her words.

"Baby, don't doubt for one second what I feel for you or for Axel. He may not be mine, but he *is* mine. I'm not goin' anywhere. I promise you on everything I have, I will be the one to teach him to ride his bike without training wheels next summer. I promise to be there to teach him to drive a car and a motorcycle. I will teach him how to treat a woman like she should be treated, by the way I treat you for as long as you'll have me."

Her hands wrap around my neck. When she pulls my head down, I see her tears falling as she begins to kiss me. We become a tangle of limbs as she consumes me.

Picking her up, I carry her to the hood of my car before setting her down. She pulls her cami off as I slide her bottoms down. With everything she has been through, I have made sure to be gentle with her. But, right now, I need this too much to slow down.

Her hands come around the waist band of my sweat pants, easily pushing them down. Taking my cock, I run the head over her pussy before I thrust deeply in her.

"Yeeeessss," she cries out as her inner muscles grip my dick like a vice. If I move right this minute, it will be over. She feels so good, too good.

"It shouldn't feel this good, but it does," she pants out, taking the words from my mouth.

"Baby…" I start to say, only to stop myself. Are we ready to go there yet? I don't know.

Sliding in and out of her wet pussy, I get lost in the sensations. With her laid out on the hood of my car, my shins and knees bump into the grill and bumper painfully, but I can't stop. Gripping her hips, I wrap her legs high around my waist, pushing her back more into my hood, allowing me to go deeper. She reaches up and tweaks her nipples. Her body shudders and trembles as her pussy milks me, her orgasm shooting through her, sending me over the edge with her.

Afterwards, we clean up and head to bed. My mind goes back to whether Fred needs to see me for closure. Making a decision, I fall asleep and rest with more peace about my past than I have ever had.

WAITING

There's no way this is my life. Shooter and I have fallen into an easy routine, a little too easy. I am waiting for the other shoe to drop. We haven't discussed Shep other than for Shooter to tell me I have nothing to worry about in him ever showing up somewhere I am. Secretly, I hope he is dead. I don't want him to get anyone else or come after me.

"Tessie, it's time to go home," Mom interrupts my

thoughts. "I'm ready to be back in my space, not living out of a few dresser drawers at Shooter's. I know he's good for you and Axel, but I want to have my own things again."

Sighing, I face what I already know. "You're right, Mom."

I am not happy about it, but it's not fair to ask her to continue on just for the sake of my time with Shooter. She is used to her space, her things. Routine is better for her disease. Plus, only having a few things with us, Axel is missing his toys as well. I spend the day packing all our things that have found their own homes here.

We are at my mom's house, trying to settle in when I get a text from Shooter that he will be home late because he is going to go see Fred. I know I am wrong for not telling him earlier. Finding courage, I pick up the phone and call him.

"Hey, baby," he greets.

"I got your message. I, ummm… We came home. Mom wanted to be back around her things, so we came back to her house."

"You moved out without talking to me?" he questions, the hurt evident in his voice.

"It's time, Shooter. You said we were safe."

"Well, fuck me for thinking we had long since moved past that. Fuck me for thinking we were building something. Damn, Tessie."

"Shooter—" I start, but he quickly interrupts.

"It's fine, Tessie. I thought something different. I get it. I made plans with Axel to go to a dirt track race with Rex this weekend, just tell me I can still do that. I don't want to let him down."

"Of course you can. Shooter, this doesn't change anything between us, only where we sleep."

"You really think it's that simple?"

"We invaded your life, your space, without asking. It was time to give you your house back."

"Did I ever complain? A house is just four walls filled with shit, but you made it home for me. It wasn't home for you, though; I get that now. Look, I gotta go. I'll see you around, Tessie. Take care. When you do Axel's bedtime story, he likes the voices. Give that to him for me please."

Before I can say another word, he disconnects, leaving me in tears. I have been waiting for the other shoe to fall and here it is. Nothing good ever lasts for me.

Four days later—more importantly, four long, sleepless nights later—Shooter is on his way to pick up Axel for the races tonight. Axel hasn't been happy since we left Shooter's even though Shooter has called him daily. Shooter may not have much to say to me, but my son is still a priority and a part of his day. Axel has missed their evening time together and the morning race to beat me to breakfast in order to avoid oatmeal. Yesterday, I even offered him cereal, and he asked for oatmeal, saying it wasn't the same without Shooter.

Hearing Rex pull up on his motorcycle, I smile when I look out and see Shooter is in the Challenger. I know Axel will be on the back of a bike sooner rather than later, but I am not ready to let go yet. At least I don't have to face that battle tonight.

I step out on the front porch, wanting to see Shooter before Axel is out here with us and he can escape.

The two men who hold different pieces of me, for different reasons, are walking up to me. Rex hugs me, while Shooter actually stands back, just watching me. Nervously, I tuck my hair behind my ears.

"I'm gonna go meet Gigi and see my boy. You two need to sort your shit. He's miserable, you look like hell, Tessie, and Axel misses the fuck outta him and the way it was. He called yesterday, asking me to fix it so y'all would be back at Shooter's. Don't make me be the reasonable one here; just talk, fuck, call it good, and make each other happy. Make my boy happy forever, and let's move on. Kumbaya, happy camper bullshit. Thanks." At that statement, he walks into my mom's house, leaving me silently staring at the man my heart beats for.

"Andy," I whisper.

Before I can move or react, his arms are around me

as his lips crash down, claiming me in a kiss that leaves me breathing heavily.

"I'm an ass," he says, pulling away and dropping his head into the curve of my neck.

Wrapping my arms around him, I inhale deeply. "I shoulda talked to you. I let my insecurities help me run away."

His head lifts, looking at me with sincerity in his eyes. He gently brushes his lips to mine. "I've been dead to the world for far too long. I went and saw Fred. You were right; he needed me. He didn't blame me. He said she had been on and off anti-depressants for years and didn't tell me. It was what I needed, only I came home to an empty house. You weren't there. Axel wasn't there. Gigi wasn't there. I've never wanted to come home to someone until you. Baby, you made me alive again."

"What do we do? I miss you, Shooter, but I can't leave my mom alone. She's worked hard my entire life to make my dreams come true, even if they didn't work out how I planned. I can't force her along for the ride of my life without considering her comfort."

"Move in with me. I'll add an addition to the house for her where she has her own space but is still with us," Shooter states calmly, like this is deciding dinner.

"Andy—"

"Don't. I've loved, I've lost, I've broken, I've

rebuilt, and I've watched everyone around me. I've watched myself. I know what I want. Your mom, your boy, and you, that's my lifeline. I've spent years shutting everything out so I don't feel. I've spent years existing, going through the motions. Well, no more. I want to spend the rest of my days making memories with Axel. I've watched your body break and heal. Now, I want to watch it grow with our babies. I want your mom to spend more time living, not worrying over you, Axel, or her health. I'll bust my ass to make sure all of you have everything you need. Move in with me, baby. Let's *live* together. Breathe with me and be with me."

Tears fill my eyes that he really wants this. Kissing him first, I then only manage to nod my head in reply.

"Okay, no kissing in front of the kids; that includes me as the overgrown child. Let's go, loverboy. We got a race to get to. Say 'see ya later, Mom,'" Rex says, coming out of the house with Axel beside him.

"See ya later, Momma. Shooter, let's go, man. It's dude time, no chicks allowed. Sorry, Mom." I laugh at my son's goodbye. Oh, my, Rex is already having an influence.

Shooter kisses my forehead as Axel grabs his wrist and tugs him away and towards the car.

"We'll sort out the details tonight when I get back,

baby. Wait up," he says with a wink before getting my son settled in the back seat of his car.

As they pull away, I can't help thinking, *There goes my heart, my world, my life.* Knowing he is coming home to me, knowing that we will work this out, knowing I mean as much to him as he does to me, knowing that my son adores him, and knowing, without a shadow of a doubt, he is everything I want for my future, I am finally at peace. There is no more waiting for the next bad thing. No matter what happens to me, as long as I have my son, my mom, and Shooter, I know I can get through it.

SHOOTER

"Why are you so on edge today?" Tessie asks, not hiding her annoyance with my demeanor.

"You don't have to go today if you don't want to," I remind her for the hundredth time.

"Are you gonna leave me there?" she asks, mocking me.

"You fuckin' know better. I'm just say—"

"Just sayin' nothing. Boomer and you go way back, and he's earned his cut. It's his patch party. I miss Corinne and even Purple Pussy Pamela. Doll will be there. Rex even said Caroline is coming. Shep doesn't get to control me. We're going to Ruthless to be at Boomer's patch party, end of story. Now, kiss me breathless."

And kiss her breathless, I do.

The small box in my saddlebag is calling for me to

grab it and just do it. My girl deserves more than that, though. I took her mom with me to pick out the pearl engagement ring. Gigi said Tessie wouldn't want the traditional diamond. Simple, classy, and filled with grace, the pearl ring with two ruby accents is perfect for Tessie's delicate hand.

It took eight weeks to add the guest house to my back deck. A covered walkway that is perfect for Claire's wheelchair is all that separates her from us. She has her own bedroom, bathroom, living area, and kitchen. There is an alarm linked to the main house so she can reach us should she need to. She gets to have her independence while still being right here with us. Her house is currently on the market.

Tessie is going back to school at the local community college this fall. With Rex now paying child support, she is still working at Brinkley's without worrying about every penny like she was before. She hasn't been back to Ruthless yet, until tonight. That's where we are going for Boomer's party.

The vote was taken at the last sermon. Boomer is a fully patched brother to the Hellions MC now. Tripp also informed us that the Desert Ghosts have been dealing with some inter-club turmoil, but received our message loud and clear.

Thorn apparently doesn't want any further problems and has given his word there will be no retaliation from them. He understands why we had to have Shep. As for his brother's behavior, he has no answer for us.

While we will never be affiliated with the Desert Ghosts again—they are forever our enemy—at least we don't have to worry about war for the time being. Tripp expects them to toe the line and warned Thorn that, if even one of them crosses into our territory, we will put every single one of them in the ground.

Pulling up to Ruthless, I don't want to climb off my bike. Having Tessie wrap her arms around me, her thighs pressed firmly against me as the gravel slides under us, is a calm I have never known. Feeling her breathing behind me, the wind blowing around us, I am truly alive again. My heart beats for her.

She climbs off, and I can't help pulling her in close to me. She is straddling my leg as I sit on my bike in front of the place that brought her pain.

Bringing my hands behind her neck, I squeeze and bring her forehead against mine. "We can leave. Go for a ride. Baby, you don't have to—"

"Shut up, kiss me, and then let's go congratulate your brother," she whispers.

Kissing her, I get lost in us, forgetting everything until the whistles sound around us. Pulling away, I run my thumb over her bottom lip.

"I love you, Tessie," I breathe out, needing her to

know, needing her to hear me say the words before she walks back inside this place.

She smiles at me, her eyes dancing with love, security, and life. She is okay. She is strength in a small package. She is perseverance. No matter what is thrown at her, she will fight through it. That is my ol' lady.

"I love you, Andy," she whispers back to me as I climb off my bike.

I squeeze her clammy, shaking hand as we cross the threshold. Getting her to the bar, I nod to Corinne to come over. I sit on the stool, positioning Tessie between my legs with her back to my chest.

"Inhale, baby. Blow out the breath. This is your family. Every patched brother in here will die for you before we allow harm to come to you. I'm sorry, baby; so sorry for what happened to you. I'm with you now, and he's gone. You are a survivor. You fought to live, and you won, baby. You won for you. You won for your mom. You won for Axel. And, baby, you won for me. Breathe, Tessie, and tonight, live for everything you have overcome."

She relaxes into me and the shaking stops. Kissing her neck, I keep my arms wrapped around her as she talks briefly to Corinne about work and life.

Taking a pull off the beer Corinne sat in front of me, I relax for the first time tonight. Across the room, I see Boomer and give him a chin lift. I am not moving and dragging her deeper into this bar, which would be closer to the room. He makes his way over with Pamela hanging off one shoulder like an extra appendage.

"Hey, brother," I greet my long-time friend.

"So, you made it for real, then? She's your ol' lady more than just as words now?" Boomer questions, not holding anything back.

"It's always been more than just words," I admit, also holding nothing back.

"Good for you. There isn't another man more deserving of happiness than you," Boomer says before squeezing Pamela's ass as she sucks on his neck, most likely marking my brother.

My phone vibrates in my pocket. Sliding off the bar stool, I take Tessie by the hand and guide her outside so I can take the call.

"Jenkins," I answer, not recognizing the number.

"Shooter, it's Young. How's the weather? Is it hot?" My old teammate, Lucas Young, replies, letting me know he needs to make sure I have some privacy. He fell off the grid a few years back and none of us have heard from him. The last update was that he took a contracted team job. I am curious as to why he would contact me now.

"I'm warm at the moment. What's happenin', stranger?" I reply, letting him know my answers will be limited, yet I can listen.

"Need a contact for a motorcycle club in South Florida. A trustworthy, walk both sides of the line type of contact."

"Hammer," I answer simply. Hammer will either help him or find someone who can.

"Roger." With that one word, the call is disconnected.

Good to know he is alive. We all have our own paths to follow.

Looking at my ol' lady, I know what I need to do.

"Take a ride with me, baby?" I ask, not wanting to take her back in the bar.

CHAPTER TWENTY

RIDE WITH ME

Mercy found it in her tonight to make that phone call come just as I was beginning to feel the walls close in on me. Stepping outside, I breathe in the fresh, outside air.

I faced the place that took so much from me. I don't know that I will ever go back to work here, but at least when the situation arises that I need to be here, I know I can make it inside. Shooter gives me comfort and courage when I can't find it on my own.

Once he finishes his call, Shooter is ready to go, thank goodness. We ride through the old country roads, just being together. When he pulls off on some random spot on Miller's Hill Road, my anxiety builds.

While I climb off the bike, he merely sits there, taking his helmet off. Following suit, I take mine off as well. Leaning over, he sets his on the ground by my feet before laying mine beside it. Taking my hand, he then pulls me to him. He pats his lap, signaling me to straddle the bike backwards and sit on his lap and the gas tank. It's a good thing I am in jeans tonight, the engine gets hot and a motorcycle is not an easy thing to climb on.

Nervously, I tuck my hair behind my ears as Shooter remains quiet, looking at me as if he is looking into my soul. He reaches up and runs his thumb along my bottom lip.

"This is the spot where you captured a piece of me. This is the spot where your car broke down. Our ride is one that's been on the path less traveled. Our journey is one of two broken souls fighting to push on. Our love is one that rises above and overcomes all challenges. This is the spot where I give you all of me for eternity. This is the spot where I hope like hell you agree to take my last name. I love you, Tessie Marie Harlow. Marry me?"

He reaches behind him into the saddlebag on my left, pulling out a small black box. Opening it, there is a pearl ring with two ruby accents sitting in front of me. "The pearl is for the grace you carry yourself with. The two rubies are for Axel and your mom. Baby, I know I'm not just committing to you, but to them as well."

"Yes, Andy, yes," I say before slamming my mouth down on his.

Breaking away from our kiss, I look over Shooter's shoulder. The road behind me is broken with loose gravel. It is in a remote area full of nothingness. The path in which it leads to is full of uncertainty. This road that has been the path of my life has been full of trials, pain, and endurance. My ride has been surviving from one hit to the next without feeling, just going on until the next thing comes. Like the road I stare at, it is behind me when I leave here tonight.

In Shooter's arms, I don't need to know the road ahead of me. In his arms, I know I am on solid pavement. At times we may find the road gets bumpy, but in his arms, I am safe. In his arms, I am complete. In his arms, I am confident in my future. In his arms, I am alive and I am loved.

REX

Ruthless is packed tonight as everyone celebrates Boomer patching in. Going behind the bar, I smack Corinne's ass as I reach down and grab a bottle of Kentucky Whiskey. She turns around to me, and I wrap my hand around the back of her head, pulling her in for a sloppy kiss.

She relaxes under me, letting me know I could take her to the stockroom right now and fuck her. The stockroom...

Jerking away from Corinne, I back away quickly. I can't do this anymore.

Uncapping the bottle, I take a swig, letting the burn permeate all the way down. Tessie was here earlier. I didn't get a chance to check on her before Shooter was leaving with her. He is everything she needs and deserves. Taking another gulp, I crave the numbness I plan to find at the bottom of this bottle.

Tessie is the strongest broad I have ever known. Shooter bought the ring, and I hope he proposes soon. She deserves her happily ever after, white picket fence, prince charming shit. I did her wrong for way too long.

Axel is the best thing to come out of all of this. He teaches me so much about myself. I have to be better and do better for him. There is more to my life now than booze, brothers, broads, and bikes. I am a dad. I have a real impact on someone's life.

Caroline is here tonight with Doll. She is once again over dressed, but I have come to learn that is her style. She has no clue about the sick fuck she is dealing with at work. She was uncomfortable and asked Doll for Tripp to look into it. Tripp looking into it equals telling me.

If she would be a little nicer to me and actually fucking listen to me when I say he is dangerous, this would be much easier. She keeps saying she has it under control. Why don't women ever listen to their intuition? She was bothered enough to call Doll in the first place, but now she is refusing help.

Another drink, more burn, but not enough to distract me from the thousand thoughts running through my head. I failed Tessie. I left her that night and he got to her.

Caroline may find me beneath her fancy lifestyle. Hell, she may hate me. However, I won't make the same mistake twice. I won't fail her. I will lay down my life before anything happens to her.

She walks over to me with Doll, taking me out of my thoughts.

"Thought you were out of town?" Caroline questions.

I drove through the night to get back here, not only for Boomer's party, but to check on Caroline. The information on this guy we got back has me on edge. She is here, safe tonight, so I can relax for the moment.

The alcohol buzzing through my system, I tease her. "It was a long ride. A ride that brought me right here to you, Lux."

~The End~
Until The Next Ride...

I hope you enjoyed *Merciless Ride*! I would love to hear what you thought about *Merciless Ride (Hellions Ride 3)*. If you have a few moments to leave a review, I'd be very grateful. Don't want to miss a single release or update to my schedule, sign up for my newsletter here! I promise I won't spam you. I send out a monthly update on my release schedule and a quarterly

Steals and Deals email full of bargain books waiting to fill your library.

CHARACTERS THAT CROSSOVER FROM THIS BOOK

The Desert Ghosts MC, Thorn, Preacher, and Shep are used with permission from Author Theresa Marguerite Hewitt. Look for Ricochet, book one of her new series coming soon.

The Savage Outlaws MC, Bowie, Tin Man, Lock, and Shay are used with permission from Author Emily Minton. Be on the lookout for Beautiful Outlaw, where you can meet the Savage Outlaws MC.

Lucas Young used with permission from author Jessie Lane. Meet Lucas Young and team in Secret Maneuvers available now through all major retailers. Be on the lookout for more Ice, Hammer, and Young in Stripping Her Defenses (Ex Ops Series)

The Regulators MC series co-written by Chelsea Camaron and Jessie Lane is now available in Ice, Hammer, and Coal.

ABOUT THE AUTHOR

USA Today and *Wall Street Journal* bestselling author Chelsea Camaron is a small town Carolina girl with a big imagination. She's a wife and mom, chasing her dreams. She writes contemporary romance, romantic suspense, and romance thrillers. She loves to write about blue-collar men who have real problems with a fictional twist. From mechanics, bikers, oil riggers, smokejumpers, bar owners, and beyond she loves a strong hero who works hard and plays harder.

Chelsea can be found on social media at:
Facebook: www.facebook.com/authorchelseacamaron
Twitter: @chelseacamaron
Instagram: @chelseacamaron
Website: www.authorchelseacamaron.com
Email chelseacamaron@gmail.com
Subscribe to Chelsea's newsletter here: http://bit.ly/2khmTzR
Join Chelsea's reader group here: http://bit.ly/2BzvTa4

ALSO BY CHELSEA CAMARON

Love and Repair Series:

Crash and Burn

Restore My Heart

Salvaged

Full Throttle

Beyond Repair

Stalled

Hellions Ride Series:

One Ride

Forever Ride

Merciless Ride

Eternal Ride

Innocent Ride

Simple Ride

Heated Ride

Ride with Me (Hellions MC and Ravage MC Duel with Ryan Michele)

Originals Ride

Final Ride

Hellions Ride On Series:

Hellions Ride On Prequel

Born to It

Bastard in It

Bleed for It

Breathe for It

Bold from It

Brave in It

Broken by It

Brazen being It

Better as It

Brash for It

Boss as It

Blue Collar Bad Boys Series:

Maverick

Heath

Lance

Wendol

Reese

Devil's Due MC Series:

Serving My Soldier

Crossover

In The Red

Below The Line

Close The Tab

Day of Reckoning

Paid in Full

Bottom Line

Almanza Crime Family Duet

Cartel Bitch

Cartel Queen

Romantic Thriller Series:

Stay

Seeking Solace: Angelina's Restoration

Reclaiming Me: Fallyn's Revenge

Bad Boys of the Road Series:

Mother Trucker

Panty Snatcher

Azzhat

Santa, Bring Me a Biker!

Santa, Bring Me a Baby!

Stand Alone Reads:

Romance – Moments in Time Anthology

Shenanigans (Currently found in the Beer Goggles Anthology

She is …

The following series are co-written

The Fire Inside Series:

(co-written by Theresa Marguerite Hewitt)

Kale

Regulators MC Series:

(co-written by Jessie Lane)

Ice

Hammer

Coal

Summer of Sin Series:

(co-written with Ripp Baker, Daryl Banner, Angelica Chase,
MJ Fields, MX King)

Original Sin

Caldwell Brothers Series:

(co-written by USA Today Bestselling Author MJ Fields)

Hendrix

Morrison

Jagger

Stand Alone Romance:

(co-written with USA Today Bestselling Author MJ Fields)

Visibly Broken

Use Me

Ruthless Rebels MC Series:

(co-written with Ryan Michele)

Shamed

Scorned

Scarred

Schooled

Box Set Available

Power Chain Series:

(co-written with Ryan Michele)

Power Chain FREE eBook

PowerHouse

Power Player

Powerless

OverPowered

EXCERPT FROM ETERNAL RIDE

Two people once lost.
Two people once broken.
Two people who have endured the pain.

One love brought them together. One love healed their hearts and made them whole again. One love carries them through both the good times and the bad.

Shooter and Tessie have faced the shadows and demons that haunt their souls. They have built their life together on a solid foundation of love, friendship, and understanding. The only thing they haven't done is make it official.

Join them as they come together to commit to one another for the eternal ride.

Continue the ride with the Hellions MC in Eternal Ride here!

ETERNAL RIDE

SHOOTER

"A re you sure I shouldn't at least go back to work at Brinkley's?" Tessie asks in all sincerity.

Sincere or not, I look over to her from our kitchen table as if she has two heads. It is the same fight we have month after month.

After she agreed to move in with me, she took time off to help her mom adjust and be at home more for Axel. Brinkley's has told her she can come back to work anytime, but that is a decision I leave solely up to her.

"Baby, come here."

She walks over slowly. When she is close enough, I reach out and pull her to my lap.

"Why do we keep having this conversation?"

"I don't know," she whispers. "Maybe because I'm

stubborn." She bites at her bottom lip, making my dick twitch in my jeans. God, she is even sexy in sweats and an old tank top. The littlest things turn me on with this woman. Hell, if I am honest, everything about her turns me on.

"You wanna work, then work. You wanna stay home with your mom and Axel, stay home. Baby, you're on the bank account; you see the statements. We aren't rich, but we damn sure don't struggle."

"That's your money, Shooter," she states calmly, just like she does every time we discuss money.

My anger rises yet again over this same topic.

"Tessie, is that my ring on your finger?"

"Yes," she answers, looking down at her left hand.

"Is it my last name you will soon have?"

"Yes, Shooter." She blows out a frustrated breath.

"Am I a man?"

"Andy," she chastises my smartass remark.

"Baby, am I a man?" She nods at me. "Am I your man?"

"Yes, Shooter, you know all this."

"Then tell me, why is it such a problem for me as a man to take care of you as my woman? To take care of my family? Are we not building something to be a family?" I watch her, trying to gauge where her head is.

"Yes, Shooter. It's just hard. I'm so used to doing it all. It's hard to accept help."

Jumping up from my chair, I stand her on her feet.

"Help!" I roar at her. She flinches, not used to me getting so worked up. "Fuck, Tessie! This isn't help. This is us being together. Dammit, I take care of what's mine. Last I checked, you are fuckin' mine. Unless something's changed that you need to tell me about ..."

Without a word, she rolls up on her tiptoes and kisses me. My frustration only adds to the passion as I suck hard on her bottom lip before pulling away, releasing her mouth with a pop.

"Baby, if you need to work, then work. But, please, stop the shit over money. I get it, baby, I really do. Don't call what I do help, ever. It's not help; it's being a man."

"Okay, Shooter."

"Okay, Shooter? That was a little too easy." I raise an eyebrow at her.

"I am yours, and you're the type of man to take care of what's yours. So I need to decide if I want to work for me and not about the money."

"You gonna marry me sometime soon, then?" If she is going to concede so easily over the money, then now is the time to push my luck on the other topic we have not quite been seeing eye-to-eye on.

The wedding. The wedding that I want to happen, like yesterday. Although the road to get us here was far from easy, I have never wanted something so much in my life—to have her carry my last name, to have her carry my babies, and most importantly, to have her share my life for always.

"Shooter," she whines, knowing this is yet another topic we will go in circles over.

"What? I want you to have my name, have my babies, and sooner rather than later. Just sayin'." I try to look innocent, but I seriously doubt she finds any of this innocent on my end.

"So, take me to the court house. I told you this already."

Exasperating woman.

"We are not getting married at the damn court house. First, I tend to avoid court houses. I don't know any Hellion that will willingly go to one. Nor do I want one of the happiest days of our lives to be at a court house. That doesn't work for me, Tessie. Second, your mom had one daughter. Baby, little girls dream of the dress, the man, the day, and so do their moms. What's the problem with you having all that?"

She sighs. "Shooter, weddings are expensive."

"Fuckin' money. Why does everything come back to money, Tessie? I may not be rich, but damn, I'm not poor."

She reaches up, placing her hands on my chest. "Shooter, this isn't about your money. I know you provide well for us. I know you want to give me the wedding of my dreams. It honestly has nothing to do with you. It's me, Shooter. I can't see spending some crazy amount of money on one day, even if it is the biggest day of my life outside of having Axel."

Tears pool in her eyes. God, I hate when she cries.

"There was a time not so long ago when I counted pennies just to get by. There was a time when, yes, I went to the grocery store to use the coin machine just to be able to get milk and cereal for Axel." As the tears fall, I reach up and run my thumbs under her eyes to wipe them away. "I can't forget my struggles, Shooter. You make everything feel so easy it scares me sometimes. You take care of me in a way I've never been taken care of before. Even when I was a kid with Momma, we struggled. I've never known how to relax and not worry about having enough to get by until my next night with good tips or my next paycheck."

"What can we do so we aren't at the court house, but you don't feel like you're breaking the bank? Tell me what you want."

"I want memories. I want family, friends, you, me, and Axel to have this together. I don't want a church. I don't want some big shindig. I just want simple."

"Baby, if it's memories you want, it's memories you'll get."

ACKNOWLEDGMENTS

Thank you first to every reader who has ever taken a chance on me. Without you, I would not be where I am today. Without you, I could not continue to chase my dream. Thank you for buying, reading, reviewing, and following. Every single one of you mean something to me.

To my hubbub- my partner in crime, love you misterman, beyond forever.

To my family and my kiddos- thank you for believing in me.

Asli, Alizon, and Kris- thank you for your dedication to making me work at becoming a better writer. Thank you for polishing up my simple idea into something magnificent.

Jenn- some days you are my brain reminding me what day of the week it is. Thanks for all you do.

Amy- you make me smile and push through… classic cars always make a man hotter.

Theresa- D4LB, oh how I love thee, let me count the ways. Thank you for our daily chats.

Crystal- the ups, the downs, the twists, the turns, thanks for being right beside me on the ride.

Emily- Thank you for the inspiration, the cross promotion, and all the laughs we share. Can't wait for everyone to meet Bowie and crew.

Laramie- you always know just when I need the added encouragement. Thank you for always being real!

Carol and Sav- this series belongs to you as much as it does me. Thank you both for pushing me into it.

Suz- thank you for always checking on me and your awesome goodies.

Sue Banner- I do not have words to express how much I appreciate your encouragement. You make me smile and keep me level headed when I want to do nothing more than give up.

Twinkie, Ding Dong, Ho-ho, and all the book whores- thanks for the laughs.

Boomer – YOU ARE AWESOME!!! Thank you for being you!

Mel- my computer says thank you that it is not buried in the back yard. Thank you for just getting me and my lack of patience for anything technical.

Halos and Horns Book Blog- Tracie- sorry sweets,

you just aren't ol' lady material. Just kiddin' you know I love your crazy, nuff said.

Elle, Heidi, Suzanne, Glenna, and my other author friends who get just as excited for another Hellion release as I do. Thank you for the support and encouragement.

Reading Renee- thanks for taking the time to read yet another one of my books. Thanks for all you do for all authors alike.

The girls of Love Between the Sheets Promotions- I cannot say thank you enough for making my release day promotions so easy. Thank you for all the time and work you put into my sign ups, my packets, my ARCs, and following the posts. You guys are the best.

Tonya and Amy from Turn the Page – For all your awesomeness, Thank you.

CPSIA information can be obtained
at www.ICGtesting.com
Printed in the USA
LVHW051930080321
680888LV00012B/1679